Declaring Spinsterhood

Declaring Spinsterhood

By

JAMIE LYNN BRAZIEL

PUBLISHED BY

amazon encore

Text copyright ©2010 Jamie Lynn Braziel
All rights reserved
Printed in the United States of America

This work was previously self published, in a slightly different form, in 2008

Published by AmazonEncore
P.O. Box 400818
Las Vegas, NV 89140

ISBN-13: 9781935597544
ISBN-10: 193559754X

~⌒~

To Mom and Dad,

without you, this would not have been possible.

To my family and friends,

thanks for the inspiration.

To www.NaNoWriMo.org,

thanks for the motivation.

~⌒~

Chapter One

IT WAS THE wedding of my dreams. As I stood in the foyer of the church awaiting my musical cue, I could not believe how smoothly the day had progressed. The weather was perfect; my constant prayers to God in the last two months for a not-too-hot Texas summer day must have paid off. All the bridesmaids had made it to their various hair, makeup, and nail appointments on time, and none of the groomsmen looked as if they had spent a wild night out—although I couldn't say that of the groom because I had not seen him yet.

The church was filled with our closest friends and family. Every pew, candelabra, and altar rail was draped with crimson roses, gardenias, and ivy. The bridesmaids wore dresses the same color as the roses; red is flattering to pretty much everyone, thank goodness. I had had my share of unflattering nightmares with horribly ugly bridesmaid dresses. I remembered one particularly awful creation in the palest shade of mint green, which with my fair skin made me look completely washed out and ill.

My reverie was interrupted by the opening strains of Pachebel's Canon in D. I loved this music and usually found it very soothing. Today, it caused a massive eruption of nervous butterflies in my stomach. As the doors to the sanctuary were opened wide before me, I stepped into a sea of faces with all eyes turned on me. The scent of all the flowers was almost nauseating. *Please don't let me trip. Please don't let me puke.* This was my mantra as I slowly walked to the beat of the music with my eyes focused straight ahead and a smile plastered on my face.

I shifted my eyes to the right and saw him, the only man I had ever loved. He was so handsome with golden hair and the bluest eyes I had ever seen, and his tuxedo looked like it had been made just for him. As I stared, he gave me a little wink. A fierce stab of emotion pierced my heart as I reached the end of the aisle and took my place on the left.

Our eyes met again as the music stopped. A rustling whispered through the church as the strains of the "Bridal Chorus" blasted triumphantly from the organ and the people turned to see the bride. Although it was the wedding of my dreams, it wasn't mine. I turned away from my brother's best man and closed my eyes as all the might-have-beens raced through my mind. Every time I thought I had put the past behind me, he showed up and reminded me how much it could still hurt.

Hold it together, Emma. You're the maid of honor, for goodness sake, I said to myself. The MOH certainly couldn't look like she'd just been gutted. I took a deep breath, opened my eyes, made sure the smile was still plastered, and focused on my new sister-in-law. Anne had become like a sister to me in the last several months as I helped her plan and coordinate the wedding. She was beautiful in her white satin gown and veil with the bouquet of crimson roses at her waist and her long blonde hair swept up into an elegant chignon.

I chuckled quietly as I took a good look at the groom. My darling little brother looked as though he'd won the

Masters Golf Tournament. Seeing how happy Teddy was at that moment, I forgave him instantly for his choice of best man, a.k.a. the man who had broken my heart. I couldn't really blame Teddy for that, though, because I had never told him the truth about what had happened. He would have killed Steve. Teddy had always been overprotective of me when it came to my boyfriends.

"Dearly beloved," my father opened. Anne knew that my dad did not enjoy officiating at wedding ceremonies, and he usually kept them short at fifteen minutes. He'd dealt with enough crazy brides to know that one slip or stutter of the tongue could bring down a world of pain on the minister's head. However, Anne had specifically requested that he use the longest ceremony possible. "After all, I'm only going to get to wear this dress once," she had said. He managed to drag it out to an hour with some creative maneuvering, but it seemed like only a second until the happy couple was announced, and we were making our final walk back down the aisle.

I wanted to do nothing more than go home and fall into bed, but as MOH, I certainly couldn't desert the bride. As soon as all of the guests had been packed off to the reception, we had an endless round of photographs taken in every conceivable combination of bridal party and family. Finally we made it to the reception hall for cake and punch. Kathy Fortner met me at the entrance to the hall.

"Honey, you look beautiful," she gushed as we exchanged a quick hug. I first met Kathy when interviewing for an assistant at my bookstore. She was a bubbly, curvy blonde in her early forties, and nothing ever seemed to get her down.

As soon as she had walked through the door, I knew she would quickly become one of my best friends, and she had.

"Thanks. At least I didn't stumble." I wasn't known for my gracefulness.

"It was perfect. You looked a little green when you first saw Steve, but I'm sure no one else noticed."

I grimaced at the memory. Kathy was aware of exactly what had happened between me and Steve. She had met him a couple of times at my family's functions, and she'd never liked him. Something about Steve had always rubbed Kathy the wrong way. She never could explain it and resorted to, "It's just a feeling I have," when asked.

"I wish the earth would open up and swallow him," I sighed.

She cackled and would have said more, but we were soon surrounded by people intent on having conversations about how beautiful the service was, how beautiful the flowers were, how beautiful the bride was, how lucky the groom was, and when was I getting married?

Inevitably, this was the first question I was asked by any of my family members every single time they saw me. I was the topic of endless family discussion because I was thirty and still single; although they didn't say so, I was always left with the impression that they thought there must be something wrong with me. This constant berating about my singleness had begun the day I turned sixteen and was considered old enough to date. My uncle Richard had led the charge with, "When are you going to find a boyfriend?" His questions had only gotten worse over the years, and he wasn't the only one who couldn't let it alone. My parents were running a close second and third.

I was having yet another one of these conversations with Aunt May when I felt a slap on my back that nearly knocked the breath out of me. Kathy had extricated herself and headed for the punch bowl.

"Well," began Uncle Richard, "I guess your younger brother beat you to the altar." Leave it to Uncle Richard to state the obvious in the most obnoxious of ways. "You ain't no spring chicky anymore, girl." Yes, he had actually called me *chicky*; what a total caveman. "When are we going to see you catch a husband, or do you swing the other way?"

I excused myself without responding, fuming and ready to throttle the next family member in my path who said anything about my lack of a relationship. As I turned, I nearly plowed into Kathy, who had been coming to bring me some punch and had overheard dear Uncle Richard's last remark. She took one look at my face and murmured, "Let's go to the ladies' room." She handed me the glass of punch and followed as I stalked off. I sincerely hoped it was spiked for my sake.

"I'm fed up with them!" I raged as I paced in front of the stalls. "They just can't leave it alone. I've dealt with this for fourteen years, and I'm sick of all of them. It's gotten to where I hate the holidays because it's the same thing over and over. 'Why don't you have a boyfriend? When are you going to get married? When are we ever going to get grand-kids?'" I wanted to pull my hair in frustration, but I couldn't risk disheveling the hundreds of bobby pins that were keeping my curls in submission.

"I'm sure they only mean it in a good way—that they want you to be happy," Kathy said. "They just don't want you to be lonely."

"I'm not lonely; I don't even think about feeling or being lonely unless I've spent thirty minutes with them. Then I'm so mad I just want to play darts with our family photograph." I took a gulp of punch. Dang teetotalers! It wasn't spiked, and I really hadn't expected it to be.

She patted my back in sympathy. "You know they're not going to change. Just try to ignore them at least for the next hour or so."

I leaned against the counter and crossed my arms. "You don't know how hard that is. It would be one thing if it was just Uncle Richard, but it's not. It's the whole family, and they don't know when to shut up." I took a deep breath. "But I'll try for Anne's sake."

I should have stayed in the bathroom. It was time for the bouquet throw, and my mother was making a beeline for me across the hall just as fast as her skirt would let her. "Emma, it's time to catch the bouquet. Don't hide in the back like you did last time. I want you up front. Make an effort this time." Dad sauntered up behind her grinning.

What is it about the bouquet toss at a wedding that turns women into animals? Do they really think that catching the bouquet has some kind of magic that makes a man fall in love and propose so they can get married next?

I placed my hands on my hips and tried to stare her down. "Why don't you go catch it for me, Mother, since you're so concerned about it?"

"Don't sass your mother, Emma," Dad chimed in while wagging his finger. "You're not so old that I can't put you over my knee."

It didn't matter how hard I was trying to get away from her, Mother was right behind me pushing me up to the front of the group that had gathered in the middle of the hall. Her scowl left no doubt in my mind that if I didn't catch it this time, there would be hell to pay for months to come.

Anne turned her back and counted to three. The bouquet made a graceful arc right toward me. I managed to jump and grab it while avoiding the stampede at the same time. Some of the other women weren't as fortunate and had to be extricated from the pile of arms, legs, and taffeta. I turned to Anne and mouthed a silent *thank you*. She just smiled and nodded.

My mother was having hysterics on the sidelines. "She did it! She did it!" she kept yelling while jumping up and down. I caught a glimpse of Kathy trying to hide her laughter behind a potted plant.

"Mother, calm down. You're making a fool of yourself." I thrust the bouquet into her hands. "Here, take the crazy thing. I'm getting some more punch."

I turned and ran smack into the last person I wanted to see. Once again my heart gave a yelp of pain, although it was smaller this time. He caught me against his chest as I stumbled. I got my feet back underneath me, but he only tightened his hold.

"You've been avoiding me," Steve said in that velvety smooth voice with the gorgeous smile that never failed to make my stomach do flip-flops.

I extricated myself from his grasp as gracefully as I could in order to avoid causing a scene. "I have not; I've just been busy helping with the wedding and all." I glanced over his shoulder and saw Anne gesturing across the room. "I'm sorry, but Anne's waving me over. I better go see what she wants."

As I turned to walk away, he let out an exasperated sigh. "There you go, running away again."

I stopped dead in my tracks as a flush of fury spread from the top of my head to the tips of my toes. Taking a deep breath, I turned back to him with clenched fists, just craving to punch that arrogant sneer off his face. "I seem to recall that you were the one doing the running."

He reached out with his hand to brush the backs of his fingers down my arm before grabbing my hand. "Can't you forget all that? Let's have dinner tonight and catch up." He gave me that slow smile again.

I mustered all the sarcasm I had. "No thanks. I have other plans and no desire to hear about your latest…achievement." I broke his hold and turned away again.

"Emma," he started to reply, but I had no desire to hear it.

I left him standing with his mouth open and eyes surprised. Steve was used to getting whatever he wanted, and I was now well aware of that. I was also aware of the effect he had had on me at one time, but not anymore. I hoped.

"You looked like you needed an out," Anne said as I joined her.

"I did." Sheepishly, I added, "I wanted this day to be free of any unpleasantness."

She waved away my apology. "That doesn't matter. What does matter is that you're okay. Are you?"

Her warm brown eyes were full of concern. I couldn't let her keep worrying about me on her wedding day, so I gave her a big smile and wink. "Nothing a good dose of Cary Grant and chocolate won't cure."

"Are you sure?" She was still searching my face.

"I'm positive." I placed my hands on her shoulders, turned her toward where Teddy was standing by the cake, and gave her a little push. "Now get back to your husband. He'll be wondering if he really got married today."

As she walked away, I breathed a sigh of relief. The evening was almost over. Kathy ducked from behind the plant long enough to say good-bye. I would soon be able to head back to my cozy, quiet home to recuperate. A mocking voice suddenly boomed out behind me. "Always a bridesmaid, never a bride; ain't that right, chicky?"

I couldn't help but smile as I turned and saw Brian doing his best Uncle Richard imitation. "I ought to kill you," I said, "but I'm so glad you're here." I threw my hand up to my forehead pretending to swoon, and cried, "Save me!" in my best Scarlett O'Hara impersonation.

He raised his arm as if lifting an imaginary sword. "Fear not, fair lady. Your knight in shining armor is here to keep the wolves at bay."

We both laughed, and I took a closer look at him. "Not exactly shining armor. Where have you been?" His suit was rumpled with tie loosened and askew.

He smoothed a hand down the front of his shirt, but it didn't help. "Server crashed at work, and then I got stuck in traffic." Brian worked in the information technology department at a national bank in Dallas. He didn't mind commuting, but I had hated it.

Brian had become my closest friend after moving next door about six months ago. Our houses were mirror images of each other, which was typical of the neighborhoods in our small town. They were both one-story brick boxes of uniformity with the exception of our tastes in external decoration. My flowers were alive, and his were dead.

The houses in our neighborhood were also very close together, which made being neighborly a necessity. I'd taken him my famous red velvet cake with cream cheese icing as a housewarming gift, and we'd clicked instantly. He could always make me laugh after a bout with the family, and we commiserated with each other over our many dating failures.

Brian reminded me of a young Dermot Mulroney, the actor, with those chocolate brown eyes and hair, full lips, boyish grin, and that adorable little dimple in his chin, but his personality was all his own. Much to my mother's chagrin, we'd never been interested in each other romantically. He'd been a godsend after the breakup with Steve, which had happened just a couple of weeks before he moved next door. He was also the only other person besides Kathy who knew the whole story about the breakup.

I had known Steve from the time he and Teddy had become friends in college, but I had never paid much attention to him. When I was working for the accounting firm, we hosted a Christmas party every year for some of our more elite clients. Steve had recently made partner at his law firm and had been appointed that year's token attendee. Since I was one of the primary accountants for the law firm, I was picked to show him around. As we talked, sparks began to fly; later that night, I gave him my number.

Two years later, I was expecting a proposal and got "I want to see other people" instead. When I'd found out he'd already been testing the waters with other women shortly before we broke up, my self-esteem had plummeted even further.

I was so thankful now that I had never slept with him. The temptation had been great, but something had always held me back. It wasn't just the fact that I was a preacher's daughter and was afraid of what everyone would think. They probably all thought I already had for that very reason. No, it was because sex was something I only wanted to experience with the man who would share the rest of my life. Maybe at a subconscious level I knew something was wrong. All I knew for sure was that self-control had paid off in the end.

After the breakup, I had needed to change my life drastically, and I did just that. I left my career as an accountant and opened a children's bookstore. I was now doing what I loved with the added benefit of not having to move in the same corporate circle as Steve. I was becoming a whole and self-sufficient woman. A few weeks later, I'd met Brian, and he had helped me pick up the rest of the pieces.

I'd learned a lot about him since then. He liked strong women probably because his mom was one, and he was encouraging me to become one too. I wasn't sure how far I was progressing in his eyes. Far too often, I let myself be railroaded by my family into things I didn't really want to do, such as agreeing to every blind date they arranged.

"So," Brian said as he scanned the room, awakening me from my reverie. "What's the plan for the rest of the evening?"

I put my arm through his and rested my head on his shoulder. "Anne and Teddy should be leaving soon. We have to clean up the reception hall and pull down all the crap in the sanctuary." I looked up at him with a smile. "Then you can take me home."

"Really?" he asked, waggling his eyebrows and flicking an imaginary cigar à la Groucho Marx.

"Very funny." I gave his arm a light punch. "You know what I mean. There's Anne and Teddy. Let's go throw some birdseed and see if we can't hit Uncle Richard by accident."

I felt sorry for Anne after they made their run to the car. Uncle Richard thought it was a terribly funny idea to dump a whole bag of birdseed right on the top of her head. It was going to take days to get all of it out of her hair, but Anne was too happy to care. Brian and I pelted him with all we had as payback, but unfortunately my obnoxious uncle was oblivious.

The car was an embarrassment. The groomsmen had lavishly covered it with all varieties of condoms and piled the backseat full of "toys." Mother was mortified when she saw it. Dad looked on disapprovingly, but I knew he was laughing inside. Instead of dragging cans, Anne and Teddy were dragging a pair of men's underwear pulled over a pair of pantyhose stuffed with newspaper. I was afraid to delve into the symbolism of that one.

After they pulled away from the curb on their way to the sunny Bahamas, everyone looked at each other as if to say, "What now?" There's always that feeling of deflation after the end of any celebration.

With a big sigh, I turned to Brian. "Ready for cleanup detail?"

He threw his arm around my shoulders. "Anything for you, babe. Let's go."

He found a ladder and started pulling down streamers while I started packing up leftover cake across the room. Various other members of the family were scattered around the room, quiet for once and helping to get everything back to normal.

"So who's the new guy?" Steve suddenly appeared by my side, his blue eyes flashing.

I was in no mood to deal with him. I kept working and put as much ice into my tone as possible. "Not that it's any of your business, but that's my friend, Brian."

He took a long look at Brian climbing easily up and down the ladder. "How long have you been seeing him?"

I didn't bother to correct his assumption that Brian and I were dating. "About six months now."

He turned his eyes back to me. "Six months. You sure didn't waste any time after…" His voice trailed off for a minute before he continued. "Is it serious?" His tone implied it couldn't possibly be.

I bristled. "You might say that."

A pair of arms encircled my waist from behind, taking me by surprise. Then I smelled Brian's cologne as he planted a kiss on my cheek. "You about through here, babe?" he asked.

Lord, he smelled good. I inhaled deeply. "Almost. All the streamers down?" I snuggled closer, playing this moment to the hilt.

"Down and in boxes." He playfully nipped at my bare shoulder. I looked up at him in surprise as I momentarily forgot everything but the delicious little shiver that spread down my spine.

Steve cleared his throat, bringing me swiftly back to reality. "Aren't you going to introduce us?"

"Oh, I'm sorry, Steve. I forgot you were still here." Waving my hand from one to the other, I made the introductions. "Steve, this is Brian Davis. Brian, this is Steve Taylor." They shook hands, each of them sizing the other up.

I settled back into Brian's arms. "Steve's been a friend of the family for many years."

"Nice to meet you, Steve. I've heard a lot about you." He was grinning from ear to ear.

"I'm sorry I can't say the same," Steve replied. He didn't look at all sorry. In fact, he looked furious. "If you'll excuse me, I've got to retrieve the candelabra from the sanctuary."

As he retreated, I turned and gave Brian a huge hug. "You're terrible, but thank you anyway." Over his shoulder, I saw Mother watching us with narrowed eyes. "Uh-oh," I muttered. "Mother just saw our little performance, and she has obviously gotten the wrong impression."

"You got some 'splainin' to do now, Lucy," he said in his best Desi Arnaz accent.

I put my hands on my hips. "I ought to make you do the explaining. This is all your fault. You just had to come over here and try to make Steve jealous."

"Hey, you know you enjoyed every minute of it." He smiled angelically. "I can't help it if your mother speculates about every guy who talks to you."

"I know." I sighed. "Let's go. I'll deal with her later." I threw my arm around his waist and gave him an affectionate squeeze as we walked out the door.

Chapter Two

"WAKE UP, SLEEPING Beauty," Brian singsonged as he gently shook my shoulder. "We're home." I was deep in thought after telling him about the part of the evening he had missed.

I shook my head to clear the cobwebs. "I wasn't asleep, just thinking."

He held out his hand and chuckled. "Give me your keys; I don't think you should be operating any kind of machinery while thinking."

With the dirtiest look I could muster, I silently handed over my keys and followed him to the door. He held it open as I walked inside and was greeted by my black Labrador retriever, Michelangelo. His tail was wagging ninety miles an hour as I bent down and scratched his ears. "How's my big boy?" He barked once in response and headed for the couch.

"There's nothing like unconditional love from a dog to make you feel better," I told Brian. I tossed my purse onto the counter of the bar that separated the kitchen from the living room.

"Well, I have something that might come close." He grabbed my hand and started pulling me along behind him.

"What's that?" I asked warily.

He just kept pulling. "Come over here and see for yourself."

On the coffee table was the gaudiest flower arrangement I had ever seen with a big bag of peanut butter cups and a DVD copy of *That Touch of Mink* tucked right in the middle. Laughing, I turned to see him grinning from ear to ear.

"I thought you might need a little Cary and chocolate to ward off the effects of the family after tonight." He picked up the DVD and waved it in front of my face.

I laughed and grabbed it out of his hands. "You know me too well. I told Anne this very evening that I hadn't been through anything tonight that couldn't be cured by this very thing. Thank you for being such a good friend, Brian."

He just shrugged. "You'd do the same for me." He pointed me toward my bedroom. "Go get out of that dress, and then we'll become hopeless romantics again for a while, unless you're too tired."

"Are you kidding?" I was already hopping on one foot toward the door as I removed a shoe. "No way am I passing up an opportunity to watch Cary. Give me five minutes."

My bedroom had turned into a total disaster area in the last two weeks as I had run from errand to errand for Anne. It was usually a cheerful room with sunny yellow walls, country blue-and white-striped bedding, and pine hardwood floors. Unfortunately these were obscured by piles of clothing, papers, and leftover wedding paraphernalia.

Groaning at the mess, I hurried to the bathroom and slid out of my dress. I grabbed a pair of pajamas from the closet, pulled the hundred bobby pins from my hair, and put the whole shebang up with a clip. My auburn curls had been tamed that morning with a lot of super-sticky hair-spray, and it was going to take forever to brush through it later. Leaving the dress where it lay, I hopped back to the living room as I pulled on a pair of socks. Although hardwood floors were beautiful, they could also be cold.

Brian and I curled up on the couch with the candy between us and Michelangelo at my feet. I loved this room because it was so warm and cozy. Although not new, the sofa was very soft and comfortable and upholstered in a bold, solid red. The wall opposite the sofa was painted the same red, and the other two were an antique ivory. Family pictures graced the walls in cherry wood frames to match the other furniture. I also liked that the living room opened onto the kitchen; this allowed me to talk with my guests as I prepared food.

As my dear Mr. Cary proceeded to seduce Doris Day on-screen, I pushed all the bad events of the evening deep into my psyche and lost myself in the movie. When the final credits rolled, I was completely at peace again, and the bag of candy was empty.

"They just don't make them like they used to," I said with a sigh.

"Chick flick," Brian grunted as he headed for the door. "Sleep tight, babe. Don't let the bedbugs bite."

I got up to follow him. "Good night, and thanks again, Brian. You're a lifesaver."

He gave me a quick peck on the cheek and ruffled my stiff curls. "Anytime." He grinned and added, "You might need turpentine to get that stuff out of your hair."

I stuck my tongue out at him. "Maybe I'll just cut it all off," I teased.

He glared at me in mock seriousness. "You know I'd never forgive you if you did."

We said good night, and as I shut the door behind him, Michelangelo walked to the bedroom door and waited. He was clearly telling me it was bedtime, so like a good girl, I obeyed. Unfortunately sleep doesn't come immediately just because my dog thinks it should. I stared up at the ceiling in the darkness thinking over the last few days. Seeing Steve again had been tough. I had been trying to avoid him as much as possible during all the wedding planning. I could only face rejection so many times, and I did not want to be hurt by Steve anymore.

I was certainly learning to take care of myself. The bookstore had been a brilliant idea to save my sanity, and it was doing extremely well. I was working out most days of the week, and the endorphins from all that exercise kept me from killing my interfering family. Mother was by far the worst. She had arranged for me to go on yet another blind date with the son of a friend a few weeks prior. I giggled as I remembered Kathy's reaction at the time.

"Honey, are you sure you don't want me to call you at about ten after six tomorrow? You know, as a rescue call in case the blind date goes south in a hurry?" she asked as we locked up and started toward our cars.

I shook my head. "It wouldn't work."

"Why not?" She stopped digging in her purse for her keys and looked up.

"Because no matter what excuse I gave, word would get around to Mother, and she'd be sure to set the date right back up again." I jammed my car key into the lock, opened the door, and tossed my purse into the passenger seat.

She nodded. "True, very true."

"If he's terrible, I'll just have to suffer through it." I sighed. "I hope he's not, though." I shivered at the thought of previous blind dates.

"Well, the offer stands. If you change your mind, just call me." She waved and drove away.

I'd always said that I could tell within the first five minutes of a blind date whether we were going to click or not, and I'd had plenty of opportunities to test my theory. So far, it hadn't failed me.

I had arrived at the restaurant about five minutes early and realized I didn't know what this guy looked like or how I was going to recognize him. I scanned the room and noticed a man about my age sitting by himself in a booth at the back of the room. Could that be him? Might as well go ask.

He stood as I approached. "Emma Bailey?"

Minute one: no palpitations of the heart, but he wasn't a bad-looking fellow, with sandy hair and moustache and brown eyes behind wire-rimmed glasses. "Yes, you must be Tom. It's nice to meet you." I shook the hand he offered quickly.

"Wow! They didn't tell me you were a looker," he said as we sat down in the booth across from each other.

Minute two: "looker"? This didn't bode well. "Thanks, I guess." We fell silent until the waitress came to take our drink order and give us menus.

Minute three: his fingernails were longer than mine, longer than any man's should have been. Maybe I should have let Kathy make that call.

"Order anything you want 'cause I'm buying." He smiled big enough this time that his moustache didn't cover his teeth.

Minute four: his teeth looked like they hadn't been brushed in months, and there were flecks of something brown between them. I was quickly losing my appetite. "Thank you for offering, but I insist on paying for my own meal."

"One of those liberated women, huh?" He kept scratching at his nose.

I gagged mentally. "I guess you could say that."

The waitress came to take our orders, and I asked for separate checks before he had a chance to say anything.

Minute five: ick! He obviously didn't trim his nose hair, which explained why he kept scratching. We were not going to click.

Minutes six through fifteen: silence descended again as I sat, disgusted, waiting for food that I did not think I could eat. The waitress brought the bottle of wine he had ordered, and he gulped down his first glass.

Minutes sixteen through forty-five: the food arrived all too soon, and he insisted on talking nonstop with his mouth full when he wasn't gulping his wine. He'd already moved onto a second bottle. He asked a lot of questions, but didn't wait for me to answer any of them. It didn't take him long to finish his meal while I just pushed food around my plate, and by then his eyes were a little out of focus.

Minutes forty-six through fifty: we paid for our meals and left the restaurant. He insisted on walking me to my car. "I had a really great time tonight," he said. "I'd like to see you again."

Minute fifty-one: he kept getting closer and closer to me. Then he leaned in with lips puckered. I stepped back and put my hand out for a handshake. "It was nice to meet you, Tom. I'll say good night now."

He grabbed my hand, but it wasn't for a handshake. "How about a little kiss good night." He leaned in again while trying to pull me close.

Minutes fifty-two through fifty-four: I was struggling to extricate myself nicely. As his manhandling became worse, I started to worry. He had both my arms in a viselike grip, and my heart started racing as I realized that I could be in trouble.

The parking lot was fairly dark, but luckily I had parked close to the entrance. I was just about to start screaming when a couple exited the restaurant. Their laughter ended abruptly as they saw me struggling. As they walked toward us, Tom finally let go and hurried into his car.

"Are you okay?" the older woman asked in concern.

I answered as calmly as I could, "Yes, thank you." I was shaking at the thought of what might have happened if they had not appeared when they did. After assuring them again that I was okay, I got into my car and drove straight home. The whole situation had left me more than a bit uncomfortable.

Brian had been furious when I told him about it the next day and had insisted that I take some self-defense classes or something. It wasn't a bad idea. I definitely wanted to be able to take care of myself if it ever became necessary, especially since that slime had practically assaulted me, but I wanted something that would keep someone at a distance. I had decided to take Dad's advice.

My father's years in law enforcement made him see things through different eyes. He still had friends on the force, and he was forever reminding me of the dangers to women in the world. He had encouraged me for years to obtain my concealed handgun license. Although I'd been around and handled guns all of my life thanks to Dad, I had never thought about carrying one with me all the time until after that date. I had asked Dad to help me buy a gun the next day, and I had started classes the next week.

The phone call with Mother the next morning about the date had not gone well. I had been headed to the shower when the phone rang. "Hello?"

"Well, how was your date?" she demanded.

I should have known it was her. I glanced at the clock; it was nine in the morning on a Sunday. "Mother, I'm going to see you in a little over an hour. Couldn't this have waited?"

"No, it couldn't. Now tell me how everything went." I could just imagine her bustling around the kitchen while we talked.

I sat back down on the bed. Might as well be comfortable for however long this took. "For starters, you are no longer allowed to set up blind dates."

"What do you mean?" she asked in an offended tone.

I switched the phone to my other ear so I could reach for the nail clippers. "The guy was hideous, and he tried to maul me."

"Emma, you must be exaggerating. Marilyn said he was a very nice young man." Of course Marilyn couldn't possibly be wrong.

I rolled my eyes. "Marilyn must be oblivious. I am not exaggerating, and we will not be going out again."

"You're just never satisfied. You find something wrong with every guy you go out with."

I had started to get mad. "That's because there has been something wrong with every man I've dated!"

Mother huffed into the phone. "I'm beginning to think that you just don't want to get married and have a family."

"Think what you like, Mother. I don't care anymore." I had hung up the phone, only to have it start ringing a few seconds later. I knew it was her calling back to chew me out, but I wasn't giving her that chance.

Luckily Brian had stayed for dinner after church and told her the story so well that she was soon agreeing with him that I couldn't have reacted any differently. He was amazing.

All this thinking was giving me a headache. I closed my eyes and took some deep breaths while trying to make my mind go blank.

❦

Cary Grant was waltzing me across the dance floor and whispering sweet nothings in my ear. Then he started licking my face, and his breath was not at all pleasant.

Abruptly I awoke to find Michelangelo in my face as he gave me one more lick. "Yuck, Mike. It's Saturday. Can't you let me sleep in for once?" His only reply was a bark as he picked up his leash from the floor where he had dropped it in order to give my face a bath. "I'm coming; just let me pee first, or neither one of us will make it in time."

After washing the dog drool from my face, I was more alert. My grayish-green eyes were a little bloodshot, and my hair was a frizzy cloud around my face. Great day for a ponytail, I thought, reaching for a scrunchie. The bridesmaid dress lay in a crumpled heap on the floor where I had left it the night before. *Later*, I thought as I pulled on a pair of sweats and tennis shoes. I grabbed my house keys and clipped the leash to Michelangelo's collar. He began to bounce as I opened the door. "Just a minute, Mike. I've got to lock the door." I barely got the key out of the lock before he dragged me down the sidewalk to the nearest tree.

As usual, Brian was already up and at 'em. He gave a little wave as he sauntered down the sidewalk to meet us. "Hello, neighbor. The dog's taking you for a walk again, I see."

I was trying to unwind myself from the leash. "Hey, Brian. I don't know why I couldn't have been sensible and gotten a little dog." I started to run my fingers through my hair, then realized I had pulled it back. "Oh no, I just had to fall in love with his big brown puppy eyes without thinking about what his size would be later."

Mike had gone to greet Brian, who proceeded to wrestle him to the ground. They always had to have a wrestling match, and Mike always won. "If you two children are through, can we finish this walk?" I asked.

"Hurry up, then," Brian said as he brushed the grass of his shirt. "*Looney Tunes* will be on soon."

I shook my head. "I can't believe you still watch cartoons."

"So do you," he said accusingly.

"I know, but you're supposed to be a macho guy," I scoffed.

"Hey, Bugs Bunny was the coolest guy ever."

I threw my hands up in surrender. "Okay, okay. You win. If you'll take Mike for his walk, I'll fix French toast."

Brian held out his hand for the leash. "Deal. Hand him over."

As Mike forced Brian into a fast trot with a joyous burst of energy, I headed for the kitchen. Unlocking the front door, I could hear my telephone ringing shrilly. I knew it was Mother. It was time to face the music for my brief moment of fun at the reception last night. I picked up the phone and headed into the kitchen.

"Hello?" I got out the frying pan and turned on the stove.

"Just why were you and Brian fawning all over each other in the reception hall last night? I thought you weren't romantically interested in each other, or were you just lying to me?" If she were here in person, her hands would be planted firmly on her hips.

I sandwiched the phone between my shoulder and ear to free my hands. "Good morning to you too, Mother. I've said this before, and I'll say it again. We are just friends. Brian was just playing around last night." I started beating the egg and milk together for the toast.

"It looked like more than playing around to me. In fact, it looked awful cozy. Steve was certainly jealous over it." I could just hear her brain ticking over the possibilities.

Add a little vanilla, dunk the bread, then into the pan. "Is that so? Did a little birdie fly over and tell you?" I'd always wanted to kill that little birdie as a child.

Her voice raised a notch. "Don't get smart with me. You might think you're all grown up, but I'm still your mother.

For your information, Miss Smarty Pants, I spoke to Steve after that little scene, and he was terribly upset."

Score one for me if he was. "Mother, he's always terribly upset when everyone doesn't bow to his wishes." I sprinkled a little cinnamon on the toast and breathed in the scent.

"That's not true." She was all empathetic now, with Steve at least. "He's very sorry about what happened, and I know he still loves you and wants to work things out. He's a very nice young man; he's just a little misguided perhaps."

I snorted. "Yeah, by his penis."

I pulled the ear away from my phone in anticipation of her shrieks. "Emma Katherine Bailey! I will not tolerate such language! When you can speak to me without that potty mouth, you know where to find me." A loud click ended the conversation.

I shook my head in disbelief. Surely she wasn't crazy enough to believe that I would give Steve another chance. Our relationship had ended in total disaster. Even though I had not told my family the full extent of his betrayal, just that he'd wanted to date other people, I was dumbfounded that she would want me to try again.

It didn't take me long to figure out from the succession of women he dated before and after our breakup that Steve was always looking for the greener pasture. After the initial hurt, my fiery temper had soon motivated me to start my life anew. I had risen from the ashes and was prospering on my own. Aside from the occasional stumble, I was doing pretty well. Was Mother so desperate to see me married that she would want me to just ignore Steve's rejection?

The beeping of the telephone and the smell of burning bread woke me from my reverie. As I hung up and pulled the pan off the heat, I heard a commotion at the door. Brian and Mike were back. They both came into the kitchen with their tongues hanging out and looking thoroughly exhausted—or at least Brian was.

He walked to my side and pulled my ponytail. "Honey, I'm home, and I'm hungry." He leaned down to look at the mess in the pan. "Uh-oh. That doesn't smell good."

I tossed the spatula into the mess. "It's all your fault. Mother called about last night, as I knew she would."

He grimaced. "Was it bad?"

I shrugged. "I know I shouldn't be surprised by anything she says, but she actually managed to stun me." I pointed to the pan. "Hence, the burned toast."

He leaned against the counter. "What did she say?" He took the pan from the stove and carried the contents to the trash.

I tightened my ponytail, which had loosened with his tug. "In her roundabout way, she actually suggested that I try to work things out with Steve."

Brian sat down hard on one of the stools looking as stunned as I must have a few minutes ago. "She really said that? I know she doesn't know the whole story, but what she does know should be enough." He shook his head in disbelief.

"I couldn't believe it either. I mean, how could she think a man who completely rejected me is better than no man at all? Doesn't she think I'm worth more than that?" My voice broke as a lump formed in my throat, and I turned away, fighting back the tears.

Brian walked over to me and took my face in his hands. His eyes were deep brown wells that darkened for just a moment with something I couldn't catch. Then he grinned and planted a kiss on my forehead while tugging my pony-tail loose again. "You deserve only the best, babe. You know Evelyn talks without engaging her brain half the time. She means well; she's just not good at expressing it."

I slapped his hand away from my hair so I could fix it again. "You're right. Let's see if we can salvage breakfast." I gave myself a little shake and reached for the eggs.

Brian left late that afternoon so that I could get ready for yet another blind date. I would have preferred to keep watching Bugs Bunny, but Dad had decided to try his hand at matchmaking. Kirk, the cop Dad had set me up with, had called earlier in the week to set up a date for today. He had insisted on taking care of the plans, and despite my best ef-forts, he had also insisted on picking me up. "I always pick a lady up at her door and make sure she gets back there safely at the end of the evening," he'd replied to my suggestion of meeting somewhere. I knew I'd never win that argument with a cop, so I gave up trying.

My doorbell rang promptly at six o'clock that evening. A man with olive skin, black hair, and dark brown eyes stood on my doorstep. He was very hot, and he knew it.

"You must be Kirk," I said.

"I am, but for your own safety, you should have asked me to identify myself before opening the door. I could have been a man who had been watching you for a few days and knocked on your door when I saw you were alone to gain entry into your residence. By your statement, I would have immediately known you were expecting a man but didn't know him personally. I could have used that against you."

A lecture on personal safety before any sort of hello? That wasn't a good sign. "I'll remember that in future," I said, nonplussed.

Unexpectedly he smiled. "Are you ready to go?"

"Sure." I grabbed my purse and jacket. He'd told me to dress in jeans and a comfortable shirt for our date. I couldn't begin to imagine what he had planned.

"Your dad tells me you're getting your license to carry," he said as I started toward the door.

"I am."

"You're going to need your gun."

"Tonight?" I asked in disbelief.

"Yes, ma'am. If you'll get it, we can be on our way."

I silently retrieved the gun case from the entry closet and wondered what in the heck we were going to be doing that required guns. The next ten minutes passed in silence until he pulled into the drive-thru of a Burger King.

"How do you like your Whopper?"

Oh boy. "Mustard, no onions." I didn't mind a cheap dinner as long as there was something pretty fantastic planned for afterward.

He placed our order and handed me the bag. "Dig in and pass mine over." This date was going nowhere fast. He drove with one hand and ate with the other while I politely munched in silence. Ten minutes later, he was parking at the firing range. "I thought you'd enjoy some practice with that new firearm of yours. I'll give you some pointers about how best to aim and shoot for a woman."

He had just pissed me off royally, and I was determined to best this vain peacock. After shooting more rounds at more distances than I care to remember, I had proven that I was the better marksman, and Kirk wasn't happy about it.

"How'd you learn to shoot like that?" he asked in disgust.

"My dad was the best marksman on the force, and he made sure I was acquainted with guns at an early age," I answered coolly. "I've spent many an hour here practicing with Dad before I was old enough to drive. Care to go another round?"

"No," he said shortly, slamming his gun back into its case. He was only too happy to take me home after that, and he didn't bother walking me to the door. I guess he figured I could take care of myself.

Chapter Three

SUNDAYS HAD BEEN devoted to church for as long as I can remember. Attendance had always been required, but I'd never minded. I'd always enjoyed church until Dad became a minister. Immediately it was as if my brother and I were put under a microscope, and anything we did or didn't do reflected on Dad's ministry. I tried to ignore it as much as possible, but it wasn't easy.

After working in law enforcement for so long and seeing how the wrong choices could put good people in jail, Dad had decided to try to prevent that from happening by becoming a Baptist minister. He hoped to reach people before they could make those choices. So the only other thing that changed about Sundays when he made that decision was that he stood behind the pulpit instead of sitting in the pew with us, and it sometimes took longer before we got to sit down to dinner. This Sunday was no different.

As Brian and I walked into the sanctuary, Dad pounced. "Did you *have* to outshoot him, Emma?" he whined. "Couldn't you have let him win?"

I couldn't believe it. "Dad, he was a vain male chauvinist pig who needed to be taught a lesson."

He sighed in exasperation. "If you keep finding something wrong with every man you date, you'll never get married." He wagged his finger at me. "Only one man walked on water, Emma, and that was Jesus." The old adage. "He's not available, so I suggest you find someone else." He walked to the pulpit shaking his head.

In my family's eyes, it always ended up being my fault that my dates didn't go well. They thought I was too picky and unrealistic. It didn't matter if the man's hygiene was terrible or he drank too much or his attitude toward women was terrible. The fault always rested with me. It was exhausting, and it didn't help that I seemed to be a creep magnet.

"Jeez," Brian said in an undertone.

"Tell me about it." I shrugged. "Story of my life—take two million." I pretended to open and close a movie slate to mark the end of this scene.

There were no traces of the wedding now except for the extra flowers. Mother wore an elegant violet silk pantsuit and her customary string of pearls. Not a hair was out of place in her chin-length bob. She was sitting in the same pew where we had sat for years, talking animatedly with Mrs. Clark, a longtime family friend who had come from the other side of the aisle to chat.

When I approached, Mother's demeanor left no doubt that she was still pissed. Hell itself couldn't have thawed the ice that surrounded her or bent the steel in her ramrod straight back. Mrs. Clark beat a hasty retreat, and I knew I was going to have to eat humble pie with a big spoon.

"Good morning, Mrs. Bailey," Brian greeted her. "You look radiant in that color." He was trying to butter her up for me, but I had to agree with him. With her raven hair, she'd always been stunning in violet. You would never take us for mother and daughter. My auburn curls had sprung from somewhere in our ancestral gene pool.

I faced the lion's den head on. "Good morning, Mother." She just looked at me with disdain. *Big spoon*, I thought. "I'm sorry for being a potty mouth." I cringed as Brian snickered behind me.

"Well, I should certainly hope so." She stared me down. "I raised you to act better than that."

I lowered my head. "Yes, I know. Again I'm sorry."

"I was only trying to help you, and that was how you showed your appreciation?" She reached for the lace-edged handkerchief that could always be found in her purse and dabbed the nonexistent tears from her eyes.

I lifted my eyes to the heavens and prayed that I wouldn't laugh out loud. I didn't appreciate her always butting into my life, but I couldn't say that. "You're right. I'm terribly sorry."

"You're forgiven, but don't do it again." She looked completely satisfied with herself as she smiled and tucked the hanky away. Brian seemed to be getting too much entertainment from the whole scene, so I made him sit between us. I was not looking forward to dinner.

Dad gave one of his famous hellfire-and-brimstone sermons, which I always enjoyed because I knew he truly meant what he was saying, and they never failed to keep me awake. I was always amazed that he didn't break something when he thumped the pulpit with his hand for emphasis of a point.

I admit that I was a little surprised when he had decided to quit being a cop to become a minister. It was a decision I admired because even after all he had seen, he had more compassion toward people than I did. Although his hair was now gray, his face was still youthful. It was the kind of face that people opened up to even when they hadn't felt a need to do so before.

All too soon, we were filing out of the church where people were milling about in groups making plans together or discussing the morning's sermon. I gave Dad a hug and headed down the front steps.

"Great sermon, Pastor Bailey," Brian said as he shook hands with Dad at the door.

"Thank you, son. Will we be seeing you at the dinner table today?" Dad was trying to talk to Brian and shake peoples' hands at the same time.

"No, sir." He stepped back to let some people pass. "I'm sorry to say that I have a previous engagement."

I turned around when I heard this. What engagement? He hadn't told me anything about it.

Dad looked disappointed. He always enjoyed talking to Brian. "Well, next Sunday for sure, then."

Brian nodded. "I look forward to it, sir."

I grabbed Brian's arm and pulled him down the rest of the stairs and away from everyone before turning to face him. "What previous engagement?"

"I have a date." He was pulling at his tie.

My hands went to my hips as I tried to read his face. "A date? On a Sunday afternoon? You didn't say anything to me about it." Why hadn't he?

He shrugged. "It's no big deal; it's just a blind date that a co-worker set up a few weeks ago, and since I work crazy hours during the week, today was all that worked out. We've only been able to talk on the phone until today." He was looking everywhere but at me.

"A few weeks ago?" I grabbed his tie to try to get his attention. "You've known that long and haven't said anything?" He'd been talking to some woman for a few weeks and never mentioned her?

He pulled the tie from my grasp. "I don't have to tell you everything, Emma," he snapped.

Surprised at his tone, I finally caught his eye and saw—anger? Embarrassed, because I *did* tell him everything, I felt the blood rush to my face. It wasn't just embarrassment, I realized; I was hurt deeply. He winced at my look. I turned and started away from him as he reached for me.

"I'm sorry; it's just that—Emma, wait!"

"Just go on your date, Brian, and leave me alone." People were beginning to stare. Childishly, I wanted to stick my tongue out at all of them.

"Emma, I'm sorry for what I said. Please, let me try to explain."

I started walking toward the parking lot. "You're right. You don't have to tell me everything, so why should you have anything to explain?"

"You don't understand—"

"No, I don't." I whirled to face him. "Just call me stupid for never thinking of keeping things from you, but I'll know better now."

"Emma," he said with teeth clenched.

My hands flew to my hips. "Don't you dare get angry with me! I haven't done anything to you but be your friend. Just go!" I gave him a shove, turned, and ran for my car.

Thank goodness it was fairly close. I was completely out of breath and had a stitch in my side by the time I got there. It's not easy to sprint in a dress and heels. I jammed my key in the ignition and drove home. After locking the door behind me, I headed for the bedroom and threw myself on the bed, exhausted physically and emotionally.

What had just happened? How long had my best friend been keeping things from me? More important, why was he angry at me? I just couldn't understand it. I thought we had always been completely open and honest with each other— and Brian was never angry. I think that was what hurt most; he was angry at me, and I had no idea why.

He'd been keeping things from me. Fear of rejection engulfed me as I relived that pattern of my relationship with Steve. A little voice inside my head was telling me that this was irrational, that my relationship with Brian was something different. He was my best friend, not a boyfriend. I turned my head into the pillow and cried.

I don't know how long I lay there replaying the scene over and over in my mind trying to figure out what had happened. Brian had been my safe harbor during the storms of my life for the last several months. Was that port closed to me for good?

I dragged myself off the bed and headed for the mirror above the dresser. My once-tamed curls were in disarray again, and I was not a pretty sight when I cried. I never understood why I couldn't be like those women who looked just as beautiful while shedding tears as they did when smiling. Unfortunately, not only did my eyes get puffy, but my nose seemed to swell to twice its size, get all stuffed up, and turn a bright cherry red, too. I sure could give Rudolph a run for his money.

I tried to repair what damage I could, but without cold compresses and a rubber band, it wasn't much. My stomach grumbled, and I realized I had forgotten Sunday dinner with the parents. Another strike for me. I called in for a pizza and played with Mike during the wait for it to arrive. Then we settled in bed and spent the rest of the evening watching Cary Grant woo Ingrid Bergman.

Monday morning dawned bright and early. It was time to get back to my normal routine now that I didn't have any more wedding plans to handle. Like clockwork, my internal alarm woke me at six. As I opened my eyes, my thoughts drifted to the prior night. I pressed my hands to my eyes then reached to turn on the CD player. Keith Urban started singing "Somebody Like You," and the upbeat tempo got me out of bed.

I let Mike into the backyard so that I could get ready for work. The hot shower did wonders for my tired body; then I headed for the coffee pot to awaken my mind. After fixing my thermos, I grabbed my keys and headed out the door.

Kathy had been keeping the place running smoothly while I was helping Anne with the wedding. She had already opened the store and was stocking shelves with a new shipment when I arrived.

"Good morning, Kathy. How are you?" I dropped my purse on the counter.

"Great." She put down a stack of books and brushed a few blonde wisps out of her eyes. She gave me her sunny smile, then cocked her head to the side as she scrutinized my face. "You look chipper this morning."

"Just glad to have the wedding over and the happy couple safely on their honeymoon." I started refilling the candy jar.

"When are they due back?" she asked as she arranged the books on the shelves.

"Not until Sunday evening."

"Well, things have been going really well here. I put the monthly sales report on your desk." She waved her hand toward the office in the back.

"I'll take a look at it later." I turned to give her a grateful smile. "Kathy, I really appreciate your taking care of things for the last few weeks."

"No problem. I've loved every minute of it."

That was one of the reasons I had hired Kathy. From her interview, I knew that she had the same love of books that I did, especially our love for Nancy Drew. In fact, Kathy and I were members of the National Nancy Drew Fan Club. We had decided to close up the shop for a week to attend the annual convention and network with collectors across the nation. We'd be leaving for this year's convention in Illinois in a couple of weeks.

"By the way," she added, "I confirmed all of our reservations for the convention. It's going to be really interesting this year retracing Nancy's steps through the countryside where the books are set."

I sighed, agreeing. "It will be nice to get away into an imaginary world for a little while."

She went back to stacking books, and we rehashed all of the wedding including Uncle Richard's comment and seeing Steve. I also gave her a blow-by-blow account of Brian's attempt to make Steve jealous, which she had missed.

Wiping tears from her eyes from laughing, Kathy said, "He is such a great guy; it's great that you're friends, but I really think you could be something more."

Frowning, I replied, "We're probably not even friends anymore."

She stopped wiping. "What do you mean? Did something happen between you two?"

Sighing, I told her about the fight with Brian.

"Whew, what a weekend you had. What are you going to do?" she asked.

"I have absolutely no idea." I ran my hands through my hair. "Any suggestions?"

"First of all, quit playing with your hair, or you'll have it in a ponytail by mid-morning. Second, you definitely should call Brian; that friendship is too precious to lose. I'm certainly no expert on relationships," she continued, "but I'm always here to listen." Kathy's husband had recently left her for a much older woman. We couldn't understand it, but Kathy handled it with her usual aplomb. "Leave it to my Albert to never follow a trend," she had said after receiving the divorce papers.

I gave her a hug of thanks and headed for the office. To call Brian or not to call Brian? That was the first question of the morning. I was hurt and wanted to make him grovel, but Kathy's words also were true. I didn't want to lose his friendship. I couldn't imagine my life without Brian in it, so I picked up the telephone and dialed him at work before I could change my mind.

"This is Brian," he answered brusquely.

"Did I call at a bad time?" I asked hesitantly at his tone.

"Emma, thank God. I'm so glad you called. I wanted to come over this morning, but I was afraid you'd slam the door in my face, and rightfully so. I'm so sorry for what I said yesterday."

"I'm sorry too. I just don't understand why you thought you couldn't tell me that you had a date." I leaned back in my chair and swiveled from side to side.

"It's just that you were so busy with the wedding and upset that Steve was going to be one of the groomsmen. It was stupid, I know, and I promise not to do it again."

He was right. It probably would have upset me. Irrational, but that was how I could be sometimes. Who was I kidding? It did upset me. I was so used to having Brian around that I had taken him for granted.

"I'm the one who should apologize. You pegged me again. It did upset me because all of a sudden you weren't there when I expected you to be." I took a deep breath and admitted, "I took you for granted, and I've been taking advantage of your company just so I wouldn't be alone. I've been holding you back."

He protested instantly. "That's not true, Emma. I enjoy the time we spend together, and I wouldn't trade a minute of it for all the blind dates in the world."

I laughed then, twirling in my chair, knowing how much he hated blind dates. "Okay, enough melodrama for the morning. How was it?"

"Not bad actually. She was a great conversationalist, which I already knew from our phone conversations; she's poised, very confident, and pretty nice looking."

I twirled a little too enthusiastically when I heard that and felt the phone jerk out of my hand. Poised is something I'm not, obviously. Had I heard him correctly? Had he just said that he enjoyed a blind date? I retrieved the phone from under my desk and hit my head as I rose too soon.

"Ow! Dang it!"

Kathy had turned around and was looking at me curiously. I gave her a little wave to let her know I was okay and heard Brian speaking from a distance.

"Emma, are you still there? What was that noise?"

I tried to regain my composure and put the phone to my ear. "Sorry, I twirled a little too vigorously in my chair and lost control of the phone cord. What were you saying?" I rubbed my aching head.

I heard him chuckle on the other end. "The date went pretty well, and I'm going to ask her out again this weekend."

"Oh, that's nice." Nowhere near the truth. I needed to get out of this conversation and think. "Brian, I'm sorry, but Kathy's frantically trying to get my attention. I need to go see what she wants."

"No problem. I can tell you all about it later. Why don't I grab some takeout and bring it over to your place tonight? Around six?"

"Sounds great. I'll see you then." I hung up the phone and put my head on my desk. What was happening to my happy little universe? It seemed like everything and everyone was spinning out of control, including me.

I spent the next few minutes lecturing myself. I was behaving like a complete idiot. There was no reason for Brian not to date that woman. I hated her already. *Irrational,*

Emma! Stop it! I headed for the front of the store to help Kathy work on the front window display. It was time to decorate for fall.

"Everything okay in there?" she asked as I started arranging books.

"Typical clumsiness on my part. I dropped the phone and hit my head while retrieving it. I took your advice and called Brian."

"And?"

"He's thinking of going out with that woman again," I blurted.

She looked at me for a moment and then said, "That wasn't what I meant, but that's okay. We'll start there. Who is 'that woman'?"

It dawned on me that I knew nothing about her. I looked away in embarrassment. "I have no idea." I scattered some red and gold nylon leaves a little too exuberantly.

Kathy just gave me that appraising look of hers again. "Okay, I'll leave that one alone and get back to what I meant by my original question. Did you get your friendship back on track?"

"We both apologized, and he's supposed to come to my house with takeout so that he can tell me all about his date." I started slamming books onto the table.

"That's good. Now what's this about a woman?" I explained what little I knew, and she looked at me for a minute before saying, "Don't worry about Brian. Everything will all work out. Just you wait and see." I wished I could believe her.

The morning passed quickly and pleasantly. Kathy and I talked a lot between customers, and she soon had me laughing. The bell over the door tinkled, and she grimaced. I turned to see Steve approaching the counter.

"What are you doing here?" I asked. He was the last person I expected to see in a bookstore, period, much less a children's bookstore.

"I wanted to talk to you," he said as he lazily leaned against the counter.

"About what?" Kathy interjected. "About what a cheating, slimy snake you are?" She'd moved between us, her fisted hands on her hips and fire in her eyes.

I couldn't help but smile at the picture she made standing there in front of him. It was like David facing Goliath. "Yes, Steve, about what?" I added.

He sneered at Kathy. "Can we do this elsewhere?" He motioned toward the door.

I might as well get this over with, I thought, and nodded. "I'll be back by two," I told Kathy, giving her hand a squeeze of thanks for being such a loyal and zealous friend.

As I went out the door, I set a brisk pace. I did not want to talk to Steve about anything, and nervous energy had me wired. Steve was doing his best to catch up with me.

"Emma, would you please slow down? This isn't a marathon."

I stopped in my tracks and waited for him. "Fine," I answered. "You take the lead."

We started again at a much slower pace. "Your mother tells me that you and Brian had a fight." He sounded pleased.

Mother had such a big mouth. "It was just a misunderstanding." I pulled a leaf from a tree as I passed and started shredding it to bits.

"Do you want to talk about it?" He tried to look sympathetic, but only avid curiosity shone from his eyes.

"Not with you," I growled.

"Sorry." He threw his hands up in the air as if in surrender. "Just trying to be helpful."

"Where are we headed?" I asked to change the subject. The temperature was in the low nineties, and I really wanted to find a shady place or, better yet, a place with air-conditioning.

"Why don't we go get some ice cream?"

"Great idea."

Chapter Four

THE BOOKSTORE WAS only a few blocks from Main Street. The ice cream parlor at the back of Driscoll's Drug Store had been a popular haunt for teenagers since it opened its doors in 1910, and the décor hadn't changed much since then. The long counter with its tall stools and old-fashioned soda fountains was still there, although a little worse for wear. The only thing that looked new was the frozen yogurt dispenser.

"Well, if it isn't the preacher's daughter. Hey, Emma! Long time, no see." Karen Willis, a classmate from high school, came to take our orders.

"Hello, Karen. How are you?"

She pulled a pencil from behind her ear. "I'm fine. Just working here part-time while I take classes at the junior college. It wasn't working between Bobby and me, so I left his sorry butt and decided to make something of myself."

"Good for you," I said, giving Steve a look that said, *I should have done the same to you.* He just grinned. I turned back to Karen. "What are you taking?"

"Cosmetology. I always did enjoy playing with people's hair and makeup." And her own by the looks of it. I hadn't known beehives were back in style. "So what can I get you folks?"

I scanned the menu above her head. "I'll have a scoop of chocolate almond in a sugar cone. No, make that a bowl please." I certainly didn't want to end up with ice cream in my lap in front of Steve. A bowl and spoon seemed the safer bet.

"And what'll you have, honey?" Karen turned to Steve with all the charm she could muster. I swear she was batting her fake eyelashes.

"Well, now." He leaned against the counter as she did the same. "Why don't you make mine the same?" Then he winked at her.

I decided he just couldn't help himself. Whenever anything female came within a fifty-mile radius of Steve, he had to flirt. Even so, I got tired of these performances.

Annoyed, I asked, "Since when do you like almonds? You always hated nuts of any kind."

"People change," he said with a smile and another wink for Karen.

"We'll see," I retorted. I wasn't noticing any changes yet.

We took our bowls to a booth and sat across from each other. "So how's business?" he asked. "When I heard you quit your job to open that children's bookstore, I couldn't understand it."

You wouldn't, I thought to myself. I had opened the bookstore because I had always been an avid book collector, especially anything Nancy Drew related. In fact, I owned several very rare Nancy Drew books that I usually kept locked in my safe deposit box at the bank. They were worth a lot of money, and although I had had some pretty amazing offers to buy them, I would never part with them. My aunt, Shirley, who'd also loved children's books, gave them to me just before she died of cancer a few years prior.

Books were my escape, and God knows I needed that escape after the breakup. Now I wanted to introduce a new generation of children to all the great children's series and foster a love of reading in their hearts. However, it seemed there were as many adults as children who were interested in collecting children's series books, and there was a lot of money to be made in helping them find what they wanted. Plus I enjoyed the satisfaction of taking care of myself.

I studied Steve through my eyelashes as we slurped our ice cream. Man, could he wear a suit. His clothes were always impeccably tailored to display his athletic physique, which he maintained by daily sessions at the gym. He was a successful attorney at a large firm in Dallas due to his ability to be very persuasive with juries and pretty much anyone else he met, including me. He thrived in Dallas, but I preferred my little town that was far enough north to still have some countryside instead of miles upon miles of suburbs and houses.

"Penny for your thoughts," Steve said, and I realized I had been staring at him. I just wasn't sure for how long.

As my eyes met his, my cheeks grew hot, and my stomach quivered. Gosh darn those baby blues! For an irrational moment, I wanted him to take me into his arms and kiss me until I couldn't think straight. I mentally kicked myself for still wanting him.

"I was just thinking about the night we met." I didn't bother to tell him my last thought.

He leaned forward and took my hand across the table. "That was the best night of my life," he whispered.

Startled by his words, I pulled my hand away. "Why is that?"

"Because I met you," he stated matter-of-factly.

I looked at him in disbelief. "That's a strange thing to say."

"Why is that?" he asked curiously. He sat back and casually threw one arm across the back of the booth.

I put down my spoon and crossed my arms. "Because you evidently decided I wasn't the best thing in your life when you decided you wanted to see other people." My voice had risen, and Karen was openly trying to listen to our conversation.

"Can we go somewhere a little more private to have this conversation?" Steve asked, finally looking uncomfortable.

I certainly didn't want our conversation to become the subject of town gossip, especially because it would find its way back to Mother. I nodded and slid out of the booth. As he held the door for me, his hand slid to the small of my back. Again my traitorous insides gave a leap. It didn't put me in a good humor.

After retrieving his car at the bookstore, we sat in silence as he drove to the lake. It was peaceful there, and I took a moment to enjoy the view, relaxing into the seat. We had been to this very spot on a few occasions, but we hadn't been watching the view then.

Reading my mind, he broke the silence. "This takes me back to some good memories."

"Please." I grabbed the car door handle. "I don't wish to hear about any of your romantic escapades." I stepped out of the car and, shutting the door behind me, leaned against the hood.

He came around to where I was standing. "Emma." I ignored him. "Emma, look at me." I took a deep breath, looked up, and saw pain in his eyes. "I never brought anyone here but you." He reached up, tucked a stray piece of hair behind my ear, and caressed my cheek as he let it drop. I flinched away. "I owe you an explanation about why I broke up with you."

I stayed silent. I was torn; part of me was angry, but the other part just wanted to touch him. The anger won out. "How could meeting me have been the best night of your life only to become something you didn't want two short years later?"

He ran his fingers through his hair. "It wasn't that I no longer wanted you. I can remember several nights I wanted you badly only to be pushed away when I tried to initiate something."

I glared at him. "So you cheated on me because I wouldn't have sex with you?"

He looked uncomfortable. "Of course not. I knew I couldn't be the man you needed me to be then." He stepped closer and looked me directly in the eye. "That's why I broke it off; I didn't want to hurt you, Emma."

I turned away from his gaze. "Funny, I guess cheating on me wasn't supposed to hurt, but that's exactly what ended up happening."

"I know that, and I'm so sorry." He took my hand, and I didn't bother trying to pull it back. "You deserve the best man in the world."

Brian had said something about my deserving the best too. I was exasperated that everyone else thought they knew what that was. "I'm the only person who knows what's best for me, so why don't people ask before they just act?"

He was making lazy circles with his thumb on the back of my hand, and I hated to admit that it was a comforting feeling. He ignored my question. "I just thought it would be better that way so you could move on. By the way, thank you for not telling your family just how big a prick I was."

I did pull away from him then. "It wasn't because I wanted to protect you. I kept it quiet because I was humiliated. I've spent the last six months thinking there was something wrong with me. How could I possibly move on thinking that?" I started walking toward the lake.

I didn't get far before he grabbed me. I struggled to get away, but it was useless. My muscles were no match for his. Out of breath, I stopped fighting and stood rigidly in his arms.

"Emma, there was never anything wrong with you. You're right; I never asked you what you wanted. I'm such a jerk, and I was so stupid to have walked away from you." He looked down into my eyes. "I'll make it up to you. I swear. Please, just let me make it up to you."

I stepped away from him. "I'm not sure I can do that. I'm not the same person I was. I like the changes I've made, that I'm still making, and I'm not sure if I can just forget everything that's happened."

He was quiet as we walked back to the car, but as he pulled out of the lot, he reached over and took my hand. I gave it a quick squeeze before pulling away. We had called a truce, but I wasn't sure where it would lead.

When we reached the bookstore, he walked me to the door. I turned back to him to say good-bye. My breath caught in my throat as he took my face in his hands. He leaned down and kissed me softly. My heart was pounding so hard I was sure he heard it as his lips left mine and glided over to my ear. "I love you, Emma Bailey," he whispered, and then he was gone.

Kathy was impatiently waiting for me at the door. We'd only been gone an hour, but it felt like an eternity. "What'd the jerk have to say for himself?" she asked curiously.

I recounted our conversation and watched her face change with a myriad of emotions, mostly skepticism. As I ended, she shook her head. "Honey, I don't know what he's trying to pull, but once a cheat, they're always a cheat." I couldn't help but think she was probably right.

I reminded Kathy that I had an appointment at the range to qualify for my concealed handgun license the next morning.

Kathy shook her head. "I still don't understand why you want to carry one of those things."

"I don't want to, but as my dad has said many times, there are a lot of weirdoes out there just waiting for an opportunity. Remember my hideous blind date a few weeks ago? I'll feel a lot safer with some protection."

"Well, one good thing could come of it," she said wryly.

"What's that?" I asked curiously.

She grinned gleefully. "You could always use it on Steve and claim self-defense!"

"You're horrible!" I shook my head at her, but she just cackled harder.

❦

Brian was bringing pizza, so I was in the kitchen chopping up the fixings for a salad when the doorbell rang. I raced to the door in my Garfield house shoes and pajamas, mouth watering in anticipation of pepperoni and black olives.

"Hello, Emma." There stood Steve holding a bouquet of red roses and looking fabulous in a perfectly pressed shirt that matched the blue of his eyes exactly. He must have gone straight home, changed clothes, and driven straight back in the few hours since I'd last seen him.

"What are you doing here? I just saw you less than four hours ago." It came out a little shrill because I could see Brian's car pulling into his garage. This was a nightmare. I grabbed Steve's arm and pulled him inside. He held the flowers out to me, but I ignored them.

"I came to see if I could take my girl out to dinner." He flashed a confident smile.

That pissed me off. "How presumptuous of you. I'm not your girl, and I already have plans."

He looked skeptical. "In your pajamas and—uh, slippers?"

I looked down at Garfield's stripes, feeling like a three-year-old. "It's an informal thing."

"Obviously." He snickered.

"Listen, you've got to go. My guest will be here any minute." At that very second, the doorbell rang.

Crap, I thought. This had disaster written all over it. I opened the door and was again completely unprepared for the sight before me. It was a blowup doll dressed in a tuxedo with Cary Grant's face printed on it.

"I say, aren't you a pretty picture," Brian said from behind the doll in Cary's clipped accent. He peeked around Cary's head and asked, "Forgiven?"

I laughed and started to speak when Steve stepped around the door. "Forgiven for what?" he asked.

Brian slowly lowered the doll, and he wasn't smiling. Uh-oh. "None of your business," he stated coldly, pushing past Steve through the door. "What is he doing here?" he asked me.

"I came to take Emma to dinner," Steve replied coolly. Thank goodness he hadn't called me his "girl" again.

"Steve was just leaving." I spoke in a tone that made it clear he wasn't wanted. "I told him I already had plans with you."

Steve raised his eyebrows at me. "Actually you didn't say with whom you had plans."

"That doesn't matter. I have plans, and you are leaving." I stepped between him and Brian. "Good night."

Brian moved closer behind me and waved his hand over my shoulder as if shooing a fly. "Yeah, good night, Steve."

A vein pulsed in Steve's forehead. I pleaded with my eyes for him to go away as I steered him toward the door. He looked at me and then back at Brian. A smug smile spread across his face. "I'll call you later, baby." I didn't see it coming: he swooped down and kissed me before he headed out the door.

"Keep your hands off her, you jerk!" Brian yelled as he headed for the doorway.

I turned, stepped in front of him, and held on for dear life to keep him from following Steve. His face was suffused with red as he clenched his teeth. "Brian! Brian! Brian!" Finally, he looked at me. "Let him go. Please, I'll explain everything. Let's just forget it and enjoy our evening."

Brian was far from forgetting it. "What was he doing here, Emma?"

"I'm not sure." I just noticed that he hadn't brought any pizza boxes in with him. "Where's the pizza?"

He pointed at the doll in agitation. "I had to pick up your doll before the party shop closed, so I thought we'd just call it in when I got here."

I had forgotten his gift in all the commotion. "Cary" had his arms hooked over the coat rack to hold him up. I extricated him and turned to Brian. "How did you find this guy?" I asked in awe as we headed for the living room.

"There's a place in Dallas that can have them custom made, so I placed my order for Cary here. I was going to save him for Christmas, but after the…thing, I decided to give him to you now."

"You did that for me?" I couldn't imagine what something like this must have cost, but I knew it couldn't be cheap. I took Cary with me as I walked over to give Brian a huge hug. "Thank you, Brian. I love him." I stepped back to admire the doll again. "What the heck am I supposed to do with him, or should I ask?"

Brian laughed. "I'll show you." He put one of my arms around the doll's waist and had me take its hand in mine. Unexpectedly, Brian stepped behind me and slid his own arm around my waist, cupping my hand and the doll's in his.

"Now, right foot first. One, two, three, and one two, three…" He kept time as he waltzed me around the living room. We were laughing hysterically by the second time around. Then he tapped the doll on its shoulder. "May I cut in?" He threw Cary on the couch.

"You're a riot, Brian." I started back toward the kitchen, but he grabbed my hand and twirled me into his arms. I gave a little gasp as my heart skipped a beat and then went racing. Brian leaned his cheek against mine and softly sang "The Way You Look Tonight" into my ear. I closed my eyes and let him waltz me around the room again.

As he finished the song, he pulled his head back and looked at me. His gaze traveled to my lips. My heart took off again; suddenly, this wasn't my friend looking at me. This was completely different—or was I imagining things? Whatever it was, I certainly wasn't ready for it.

"I better go call in that pizza," I said to break the spell, heading for the kitchen. After making the call, I took a minute to hide behind the refrigerator door and compose myself. My heart was still racing as I peeked around the refrigerator. Brian had let Michelangelo in from the backyard and was wrestling him. That was normal, so maybe it was just me that had become abnormal.

I pulled a head of lettuce out of the fridge and started chopping it with a vengeance. *Slow down. No need to lose a finger.* Why was I getting all fluttery around Brian? Maybe I was just hormonal and reacting to all things male. Yeah, that must be it.

I stopped chopping. Now I was feeling relieved to have my best friend at a distance. What did that say about me? *I'm going stark, raving mad,* I said to myself. *I have no idea who I am anymore.*

"Don't you think that lettuce is chopped enough?" Brian asked, breaking my thoughts.

"Yeah." I could feel my face turning red. "Would you grab the salad bowl out of the cabinet?"

"Sure." He placed it in front me and leaned against the counter. His arm brushed mine and sent a tingle straight to my spine.

"Cold?" He must have noticed me shiver.

"No, just somebody passing over my grave I guess." Gosh, he smelled good. I had no idea what his cologne was called, but it was having a very definite affect on my brain. "Excuse me a minute?"

"No problem. I'll take over here." Brian was not known for his cooking abilities, but he couldn't possibly screw up salad.

As he took the knife from my hand, the words to "Lightning Striking Again" played stupidly through my head. I was losing it and fast.

I practically ran for the sanctuary of my bedroom, put my head between my knees, and took some deep breaths as I sat on the edge of the bed. I was turning into a complete loon. *Get control of yourself, Emma. It's Brian, for goodness sake. You're just mixed up and overly sensitive because of the wedding and Steve.*

I went into the bathroom and splashed some cold water on my face at the sink and looked at myself in the mirror. There was no denying it. I looked scared to death. Of what, I didn't want to try to decide right now. Drying my face, I saw my favorite lip gloss out of the corner of my eye. *What the heck?* I thought as I applied some and smacked my lips together. I didn't have to look dead as well as crazy. I squared my shoulders, tossed the tube on the vanity counter, and marched back to the kitchen.

Brian watched me as I got the ranch dressing out of the refrigerator. "Nice lips."

I stopped mid-reach and looked at him. "What?"

"I always liked that gloss on you." He'd noticed. Crap! Or was it a good thing that he had noticed? "Makes your lips look awfully kissable," he quipped.

For the second time that day my heart stopped, and I swirled to look at him. His eyes were teasing as he grinned from ear to ear.

"Very funny." I frowned at him and turned back to the refrigerator. I must have been imagining things earlier, but he certainly seemed like the same old Brian now. To be honest, I felt a little deflated in that second.

The doorbell rang for the third, and I hoped final, time that evening, announcing the arrival of the pizza. "Can you get that?" I asked him.

"Absolutely."

"No sneaking the olives on the way back either," I called out. He always tried to eat them all before I'd had a chance to even get a slice. I put Michelangelo in the backyard so we wouldn't have to withstand his begging. I'd give him leftovers later.

Over our dinner, Brian filled me in on his date. "Her name's Delilah and she's a professor of literature at the community college. You'd probably enjoy talking to her since you both like books."

I bet, I thought sarcastically. Delilah. She couldn't be nice, not with a name straight out of a Bible seduction story. "Probably," I said noncommittally. Not.

Then he turned the tables on me. "So why is Steve back in the picture all of a sudden?"

"Well, he's not exactly." I went on to explain how tonight's train wreck had been put into motion.

"You can't possibly believe he's telling the truth," Brian said.

"Honestly, I don't know what to believe anymore except that it's all driving me crazy." We started clearing the dishes from the table.

"Emma, he was cheating on you," Brian reminded me as he loaded the dishwasher. "He was seeing someone before he even told you he wanted to see other people. Kathy's got him pegged."

"I know that, but maybe he did just have a commitment phobia at that time. To believe the opposite just means there really was something about me he didn't like," I trailed off into a whisper. I started back to the living room as Brian let Michelangelo in and fed him scraps. They both joined me on the couch.

"Babe," Brian continued, "the only thing he didn't like about you was that you wouldn't put up with his crap. That's a good thing."

I wasn't convinced. "Maybe I am too picky, like my family says."

"Would you want to settle for less and be unhappy?" he asked.

"No. I really just want to forget it all and go to bed. I'm exhausted." I wasn't really, but I was suddenly uncomfortable with him.

Brian headed for the front door, and I followed feeling like a complete heel. He looked at me a moment as he opened the door and then tousled my curls like he would a younger sister. "Off to bed, sleepyhead, and I'll see you in the morning."

I gave him a small smile, said good night, and closed the door behind him. Turning, I found Michelangelo looking up at me with his big sad eyes. "Oh, Mike," I sighed as I sank to my knees beside him and wrapped him in my arms. The only bad thing about dogs is that they can't hug you back.

Left with only my thoughts for company, they took a completely new direction. I toyed with the idea of just giving up on dating period. I knew it would mean constant harassment from my family, but the more I thought about it, the more I became intrigued. After all, I wouldn't be the first old maid to ever live. Why couldn't I learn to be happy by myself?

Chapter Five

BRIAN WAS AT my door the next morning with coffee and bagels. "Sustenance for the big day," he declared, handing me the coffee.

"Big day?" I asked in confusion. "What are you talking about?"

He looked at me in disbelief. "You're qualifying for your license today, aren't you?"

"Oh, crap. I'd forgotten." I looked at the clock, which read 8:30 a.m. "I've got to go. I'm supposed to be there at nine."

"Good luck." He started back down the sidewalk. "Let me know how it goes."

❧

I squeezed the trigger, firing the last of my fifty rounds straight through the chest of the paper target with my 9mm Sig. Satisfaction swelled through me. I could certainly take care of myself if I must.

"Looks like the apple don't fall far from the tree," the instructor said after I had removed my earplugs. "Your dad always could outshoot everyone in the department."

I smiled wryly. "Well, he made sure I had lots of practice."

"I bet. Well, you passed with flying colors. You should get your license in the mail in about three weeks."

"Great." I cleaned my gun and put it back in its case. The thought of being an old maid didn't bother me so much with the gun in my hand. Who needs a man when you've got a gun?

"Tell your dad I said hello," my instructor called out as I walked through the exit.

"I will."

On the drive home, I continued to think about how I might be able to make the spinster thing work for me. I was tired of being a dependent female always worried about what other people would think, and hadn't I already shown myself that I didn't have to be? After all, I'd started the bookstore and could certainly handle a gun. I was happy with my life as it was, and if I stuck to it, wouldn't it prove to everyone that I was strong?

I went straight back to my house to put my gun away and get cleaned up for work. Shooting was always a dirty business. Grime seemed to get everywhere. It didn't take long to wash the gunpowder from my hands, change clothes, and drive to the bookstore. The bell jingled over my head when the door opened, and Kathy popped up from behind the counter.

"Well, if it isn't Dirty Harriet!" she exclaimed. Then she laughed. "I've been waiting all morning to say that."

"Very funny, Kathy. You're a riot as always."

"So, seriously, how'd you do?" She sat down behind the counter as I put my stuff away.

"No problem. I'll have my license in about three weeks."

"Well, I still don't like the idea of your carrying a gun, especially around your mother." She laughed uproariously and pounded her knee.

I put my hands on my hips. "Have you spent all morning just coming up with one-liners?"

"Pretty much, although I did take enough time to put up all the signs about the sale."

"I'm glad to hear you got a little work done this morning," I teased.

The rest of the week flew by as Kathy and I took inventory in preparation for restocking. We were leaving for the convention next weekend, and we would be unveiling a new section of the bookstore devoted entirely to Nancy Drew. In fact, I was even bringing my rare books out of safekeeping for a show-and-tell at the children's story hour.

I hadn't seen much of Brian. Work or Delilah was apparently taking all of his free time. I tried not to let it bother me, but it was quickly becoming a nagging worry at the back of my mind.

To celebrate the end of our hard work, Kathy and I had a girls' night out on Friday. We drove to Dallas for Italian food and salsa dancing. For some reason, I could always lose my clumsiness on a dance floor. We had a great time and certainly had our share of men hitting on us.

I motioned to Kathy that I needed a breather and made my way to an empty table nearby. I'd only been sitting about two seconds when a guy approached. He wasn't bad looking, but he oozed narcissism.

"Hey, baby." He leaned one hand on the back of my chair and stooped closer. "You are smokin' hot. Can I buy you a drink or, better yet, find us a dark corner?" His hand trailed along my bare shoulder.

I shrugged his hand away in revulsion. "No thanks."

He sat in the chair beside me. "Aw, c'mon, baby. Play nice." He reached for my hand. I held up a tiny can of pepper spray that clipped onto my bracelet. "Get lost." My tone clearly conveyed that I meant business.

He snarled but retreated to the bar. Kathy was making her way to the table. "Who was he?" she asked.

I shrugged. "Just some sleezeball. Having fun?"

"Loads!" She was definitely enjoying being single again.

I smiled at her. "I envy you."

"Why?" she asked in surprise.

"Here you are, after a divorce, enjoying the whole dating scene." My gesture encompassed the whole room.

"Don't you?"she asked curiously.

"No," I sighed. "To be honest, I wouldn't care if I never went on a date again."

She waved my comment away. "Honey, you just haven't met the right guy yet. There's no hurry, you know." She leaned her head on her hand and stared dreamily into space. "Somebody will knock your socks off one of these days, so why not enjoy the variety in the meantime?" She batted her eyelashes at me.

Laughing, I pulled her back onto the dance floor and boogied like I didn't have a care in the world, but later that night I was staring at my ceiling again. I really was tired of dating and relying on everyone, especially Brian, to take care of me. It was time for me to learn to stand on my own two feet.

Sunday dawned overcast and rainy. I hated these kinds of days. They always put me out of sorts, especially because my curly hair refused to cooperate into any type of style but a frizzy ponytail. The one bright spot was arriving at church with Brian and seeing Anne and Teddy there.

"What are you two doing here?" I asked, giving her a hug.

"Well, our flight got in a little earlier than we expected last night, so we were able to come this morning," Anne replied. "How are you?"

"Better now that you're home."

Teddy gave me a huge bear hug and pulled my ponytail. "Hey, sis!"

At that moment Brian walked up. "Teddy! My man! How was the honeymoon?"

Anne blushed prettily as Teddy kissed her cheek. "I'll tell you about it later," he replied with a huge smile.

"You will not," Anne protested, becoming redder than ever. We laughed at her discomfort.

After church we all walked to the parsonage for dinner. Mother had already beaten us there and was busy preparing everything in the kitchen. As we entered the dining room, I was mortified. Steve Taylor was seated on the other side of the table, grinning from ear to ear. His smile faltered as he got a good look at my expression.

"Will you please excuse me a moment, everyone?" I asked politely and headed for the kitchen with murder in mind. I was going to strangle Mother and enjoy every minute of it.

"What the hell do you think you're doing?" I hissed at her. I didn't usually resort to curse words, but she had exasperated me beyond reason.

She turned to me as she took a pan of dressing from the oven. "Language, Emma. I'm about to serve dinner. What are you doing?"

I stepped in front of her. "How could you invite him here?"

"I thought it was high time you two talked out your problems, and he always did enjoy my dressing." She lifted the pan she held in front of her.

I clenched my fingers in my hair. "Why can't you just stay out of this? It's none of your business."

She put the pan down on a hot plate and put her oven-mitted hands on her hips. "It is my business when I know that my only daughter isn't happy."

I glared at her through narrowed eyes. "Just because I don't have a husband doesn't mean I'm not happy, Mother." I sighed and leaned back against the counter.

She started dishing up the potatoes. "That isn't what I said, but I do think you would be happier if you weren't alone all the time."

"I'm not alone all the time; I'm always with Kathy or Brian."

"I always thought you and Steve made a lovely couple," Mother went on as if she hadn't even heard me.

"Huh. Until he decided I wasn't enough for him anymore, and he wanted to date other women."

"Well, I believe he's seen the error of his ways." She cocked her head and looked into my eyes. "Give him a chance, Emma. The good Lord knows that your father wasn't perfect when I married him, but look how happy we are now. You know, Steve reminds me of him," she mused.

I snorted with laughter and reached to sample the potatoes. "Just how is that? He's certainly not pastor material."

She slapped my hand away. "That's not what I mean. I'm talking about your father before he became a pastor. He was a little reckless and wild like Steve, and he broke up with me once because he wanted to date someone else."

I gaped at her before spluttering, "You never told me that. What happened?"

She stopped her fussing and turned to look at me. "Well, I didn't sit around waiting for him to come back, if that's what you mean. No, sir. I had myself a date the next weekend and the weekends thereafter. Your father dated that other woman for a while, but he soon figured out that she was very high maintenance. She made him absolutely miserable. Then, a short time after they broke up, he came crawling back to me begging for forgiveness. Of course I made him earn it, but he was the only man I could possibly love, and he had realized that I was the only woman for him."

I watched my mother as she removed the dressing from the pan and placed it in a serving dish with a look of total confidence. I envied her at that moment because I didn't have that confidence. We had shared a similar experience but reacted in completely opposite ways. My confidence had been shattered after Steve dumped me, but I was finally putting my life back together. She wanted my story to end like hers, in happiness, but I couldn't risk letting Steve hurt me again, or anyone else, for that matter. I realized in that moment that I was going to disappoint her because I was through with all of it.

I walked to her side and kissed her cheek. "You know I love you, right?"

"I love you too, dear." She untied her apron. "Now give me a hand carrying this out." We both grabbed dishes of food and headed for the table. Dad and Steve were discussing the upcoming presidential election. *Thank goodness they're both on the same side*, I thought. Otherwise, dinner would have turned out to be a shouting match. Dad loved a good debate about politics, and I'd known him to shout down many an opponent. He'd be great in a filibuster.

Brian, Anne, and Teddy were sitting silently in their chairs. Brian looked up in concern as I entered the room, but I gave him a confident smile before taking my place beside him. I knew what I had to do.

Conversation during the meal was stilted, to say the least. If it hadn't been for Dad talking to Steve about politics, it would have passed in silence. I mainly kept my eyes on my plate in order to avoid Mother's crazy facial expressions with which she was obviously trying to get me to talk to Steve. Instead, I thought about what I was going to say to everyone in just a few short minutes.

When it appeared that everyone had finished eating, I stood up. All eyes turned to me, and I took a deep breath. "I have something I need to tell everyone." Another deep breath as I looked straight at Mother. "Today I am declaring spinsterhood."

Everyone looked confused for a few minutes, but then it began to dawn on a few of them exactly what I meant. "Whatever are you talking about, Emma?" Mother looked irritated.

"Well, since I can't trust my own judgment when it comes to dating, the obvious fact that I'm a creep magnet, uh..." I looked quickly at Steve, but he still seemed confused. "And since my family's choice of dates doesn't seem to be any better, I have decided to quit dating." I ventured a look around the table. Dad obviously thought I was crazy. Anne appeared stunned. Teddy was watching Steve as if he'd just realized there was more to the story. I couldn't look at Brian. I was afraid of what I would or wouldn't see.

Steve smiled and said, "You can't possibly think we believe this," as if I were a little girl throwing a tantrum who needed to be soothed.

I stared him coldly in the eye. "Be very sure, I mean every word."

Mother made an impatient noise. "That's just ridiculous." She stood and started stacking plates.

Brian reached up and took my hand. I held on for dear life and faced Mother squarely. "You know, it may be, but I've had it anyway. I'm happy with my life the way it is, and I'm quite able to take care of myself."

She stopped stacking and looked at me with eyes full of hurt and disappointment. "I certainly hope so, because you'll get no more help from me," she said quietly. She picked up the stack of plates and continued. "As long as you persist in this ridiculous attitude, you are no longer welcome in this house." She turned and made her way to the kitchen.

"Evelyn, wait!" Anne cried and started after her. "You can't mean that!"

"Yes, she can," I said under my breath. I was stunned. I knew she would be disappointed, but I never dreamed she would cut me out of her life. Tears welled in my eyes.

Steve snickered. "You really think you can be happy as an old maid?"

Blinking back tears, I turned to him. "At least I'll be better off than with a cheater like you."

"Cheater?" Teddy rocketed out of his chair.

"You cheated on her?" Dad asked incredulously.

Oh, crap. I'd let the cat out of the bag. Steve was stuttering as they advanced on him. I could hear Anne and Mother arguing in the kitchen, and then I realized that Brian was still holding my hand without having said a word. I finally turned to look at him and was stunned to see pride beaming in his eyes.

I giggled a little hysterically before regaining control enough to ask, "Take me home?"

The ride home was a bit of a blur. I kept repeating, "I did it. I can't believe I did it."

Brian kept telling me how proud he was that I had finally stood up for myself. "You were wonderful, Emma, so strong and confident, but are you really sure you want to give up on dating? I mean, you always said you wanted to have kids."

"Yes, I mean it. Look at me. I'm practically a nutcase already because of all this. I'd have to be better off without it, and besides, I can have kids without a man. Look at Angelina Jolie and all those other women who adopted when they were single." My voice was rising higher with every word, and I couldn't feel very victorious at that moment. I just couldn't believe that my mother had actually banned me from the house.

When I mentioned this, Brian assured me, "She's just upset, Emma. She'll come around."

I couldn't believe any of it. I was headed for a hysterical crying jag by the time he got me home. Poor guy. He looked terrified as I sobbed and giggled on the couch. "Why don't I call Kathy?" he asked, obviously wanting to vacate the premises. I nodded because I couldn't speak. He picked up the phone and explained quickly.

By the time she arrived, I was in a silent stupor, and Brian was pacing the floor. Mike was in the corner howling occasionally in sympathy. She sat beside me on the couch and announced, "I have Cary or José. Which will it be?" She held up a DVD and a bottle of tequila. I threw my arms around her neck and started laughing and crying again. "José it is," she said, patting my back awkwardly with her hands full.

"No," I said, sitting back and wiping my eyes. "I don't need you to get me drunk, although I appreciate the thought. I'm just glad you're here."

"You just need a little girl talk and forget all these men." She turned to Brian, who was hovering near the door, and flapped her hands. "Shoo! I'll take care of Emma." He left in obvious relief. She turned back to me, grinning. "Isn't it funny how they turn tail and run at the first sign of tears?"

I laughed, but I was disappointed at how quickly he'd left. He'd never run from my tears before now. Kathy pulled a bag of Reese's Pieces from her bag and handed them to me. "Now spill," she said.

That's exactly what I did. I told her all about the thoughts and events that had led to today's announcement.

"Well, honey, you're certainly not the first woman who's ever wanted to tell everyone to leave her alone, but are you sure this is what you really want?"

I closed my eyes and leaned back against the couch. "I better be because there's no taking it back now."

Chapter Six

THE NEXT WEEKEND finally arrived, and by that time, I was utterly out of sorts. Thanks to Anne's persuasion, Mother had relented to my decision although under great duress. I was enduring daily phone lectures and wheedling, but I guess that was a small price to pay for peace in the family. Steve had called every night trying to make a date for dinner, obviously seeing my declaration as some sort of challenge to be overcome. I'm not sure what explanation he had given my brother and father about his cheating, but he had obviously smoothed things over, and I chose to let sleeping dogs lie when they asked me about it.

I felt awkward with Brian after my outburst, and he looked like a thundercloud if I mentioned Steve's name, so I just quit talking about anything but the weather and work. And Delilah. Oh yes, he was going out with her again that weekend, and of course he had no problems talking about that. I said a little prayer of thanks to God that I wouldn't be around afterward to hear him speak glowingly of her charms. I needed my vacation first.

I was trying to maneuver my suitcase out of my bedroom when the doorbell rang. That had to be Kathy. She was picking me up so that we could ride to the airport together. I opened the door. "I'm almost re—sorry, I thought you were Kathy." Brian was standing at the door.

"I just came to pick up Mike for the wild party at the bachelor pad this weekend."

I rolled my eyes as I let him in. "You'll both be asleep on the couch by ten."

"Not tomorrow night," he countered smugly.

"What's tomorrow night?" I turned back to my room to get my carry-on bag.

"My date with Delilah."

I made a face while my back was turned. "That's right. Well, just remember to keep it PG in front of Mike," I said jokingly as I came back into the living room, bag in hand.

"Ha, ha. Very funny. You got his gear together?"

"It's all in here." I dropped my carry-on by the door and handed him a sack with Michelangelo's leash, toys, and treats. Brian had his own supply of dog food for occasions like this one.

He went to retrieve Michelangelo from the backyard as Kathy pulled up into the drive. I hurried out to the car and put my bags in the trunk, then stuck my head in the passenger window. "I'll just be a second. Brian's here to get Mike."

"No hurry. We've allowed ourselves plenty of time."

An exuberant Michelangelo was trying his best to pull Brian down the sidewalk as I walked toward them. "Whoa, Mike," he commanded and paused beside me. "So you'll be back next Saturday?"

"Yeah. Around five."

"Mike and I are going to miss you." He tucked an errant curl behind my ear.

I missed him already because neither one of us had been our familiar selves the last few days. I bent down to scratch

Michelangelo's ears so I wouldn't have to see what was in Brian's eyes—or what wasn't there. "I'll miss y'all too."

I stood up, and he gave me a quick kiss on the cheek. "Have a safe flight," he called back as Michelangelo tore off down the sidewalk. I retrieved my purse and locked the front door.

"Okay, what's up?" Kathy asked as she backed out of the drive.

"What do you mean?" I kept my eyes straight ahead, blinking away the sudden moisture.

"You look like you just lost your best friend."

I sighed, looking out the window. "I think maybe I have."

"Now it's my turn to ask. Just what do *you* mean?

I told her about the awkwardness between us, the look in Brian's eyes that night after we waltzed, my own reactions to it, my total panic thereafter, and finally my big declaration. "I haven't really been able to talk to him since. He just talks about Delilah." I practically spat the name. "I don't know. Maybe I'm just imagining things."

Kathy kept her eyes on the road, but didn't hesitate to let me know her opinion. "Honey, I think you're jealous."

I looked at her in outrage. "I am not. What do I have to be jealous about?"

"I think you're afraid that this Delilah might actually mean something to Brian. Now that type of jealousy could stem from one of two things. One, you're just afraid your friend won't have any more time for you or, two, you want that friend to be something more."

I spluttered over in the passenger seat. Then I stopped. Was she right? I had to admit I was afraid of losing Brian's friendship, but was it because I wanted him for myself?

"You're right in one aspect," I admitted. "I am afraid that I'll lose Brian as a friend, but I don't have romantic feelings for him. And even if I did, I couldn't possibly act on them because he doesn't feel that way, and it would definitely ruin the friendship then."

"How do you know he doesn't feel that way?"

"Please," I uttered sarcastically. "He thinks of me like a sister."

She looked at me doubtfully as she pulled into the long-term parking lot at the airport. "I've seen the way he looks at you sometimes, and it's definitely not brotherly."

I rolled my eyes. "What are you talking about?"

"It's more like Mike looking at the dog treats high up on the shelf out of reach." She giggled.

"Kathy, you're a nut."

"Honey, I know that, but if I were you, when we got home, I'd grab that man in my arms and teach him a few things about dog treats."

I burst out laughing. "Your advice never fails to amaze me. Besides, I'm an independent woman now. Why can't everything stay the way it was? Come on. Let's forget all this and disappear into mythical River Heights."

"You got it!"

❦

We managed to get in a little personal shopping on Saturday and Sunday before the convention started bright and early Monday morning. It kept us busy for the next several days with guest lecturers, book fairs, tours of the "sights" from the books, treasure hunts, and solving mysteries.

Thankfully I hadn't had any time to think about my personal problems.

Finally it was time for the farewell dinner and dance. Everyone dressed up like a character from one of the books. I was going as Brenda Carlton, the snobby reporter and rival of Nancy in the Files series. Kathy had decided to go as Nancy's friend Bess so that she wouldn't have to wear much of a costume. She already shared Bess's long blonde hair and curvy figure. I had brought a long black wig and fake nails painted tomato red. We went back to our rooms after the final lecture to get ready for the evening ahead.

"Wow!" Kathy exclaimed as she walked through the adjoining door to our rooms to stand beside me at the mirror. "You look completely different."

"In a good way or a bad way?" I asked as I applied my lip gloss. I had donned my wig and an emerald green satin halter dress that made my eyes stand out. My toenails, also painted red like my fake "Fire Engine" fingernails, peeked from beneath the hem of my dress inside black strappy heels. "Hooker heels," Mother would have called them.

"Definitely in a good way. You should consider changing your hair color to black. That would definitely get the men in your life stirred up." Kathy was laughing now.

"They're stirred up enough, thank you very much," I answered wryly, looking in the mirror as I applied another coat of mascara. I definitely looked different, and it was fun to be in disguise. I had to admit that, dressed like this, I felt downright sexy.

I turned to get a better look at Kathy's outfit. "You're going to turn some heads yourself tonight," I told her. She looked fabulous in a sapphire blue dress that could have come straight out of the fifties.

She twirled. "You like it? I got it from a vintage clothing store."

"It's beautiful, and I love your hair." She had pulled it up into a high, curly ponytail, and her bangs were swept to the side.

"Thanks. You ready to boogie?" She twitched her hips from side to side.

"Let's go."

The conference hall had been turned into a buffet area on one side with the dance floor on the other. The band on stage was playing a fast swing number as couples danced the quick step. We could see several women dressed up as Nancy, Bess, and George, but I was definitely the only Brenda. A lot of the men were dressed as Nancy's dad, Carson.

We found our assigned table and looked at the place cards for our names. As I approached my seat, a man rose from the place next to mine and pulled out my chair. His gaze wandered from the top of my head to my peek-a-boo toes and back again. He was tall and muscular without being overly so. He had light brown hair and the softest brown eyes with flecks of amber near the pupils.

"Hello," he said as he took his seat again after helping Kathy with her chair. "My name is John Delancey." He turned those wonderful eyes back to me.

I sat dumbfounded; this man perfectly fit the description of Nancy's boyfriend, Ned Nickerson, whom I had fantasized about as a young teenager. It was uncanny. Kathy gave me a nudge.

"My name is Kathy Fortner, and this is Emma Bailey," she said over my shoulder. "Spinster, huh," she whispered in my ear, and I blushed as I realized that I had been openly staring and silent.

"It's a pleasure to meet you both." He smiled, showing perfectly even and beautifully white teeth."What area are you from?"

"We're from Texas," I said, finally having regained control of my tongue. "And you?"

Before he could answer, a very distinguished looking "Carson" asked Kathy to dance, and they left the table together.

"I currently reside in New York, but I do a lot of traveling for my job," John continued. "I help facilitate the exchange of collectible items between parties."

"Is that what brought you to the convention?" I asked out of curiosity.

"Yes. One of my clients is interested in purchasing first edition Nancy Drew books that are few and far between." He went on to describe the books.

"I have some of those in my collection at home!" I exclaimed.

"Really?" His eyes lit up in anticipation. "Would you be willing to part with them? The price is very good."

I shook my head. "No, not at any price. They have great sentimental value to me. They were given to me by my favorite aunt just before she passed away."

"Well, if you should change your mind, please call me." He handed me a business card, and a jolt of electricity shot up my arm as our hands met. "Of course, you could call me even if you don't change your mind." He smiled as I blushed yet again.

"So tell me more about your collection," he continued, trying to distract me from my discomfort. I did so with enthusiasm; I always loved talking about books. John listened intently and asked a lot of questions, especially about the rare books.

When I finished, he smiled and said, "Your love of books is evident in the way you describe them. I admire that."

"Thank you." I took a sip of water and saw that my hand was trembling a little. Moving on to other topics, we found that we had a lot in common, like our love for animals, eclectic tastes in music, and love of good Italian food. Before we knew it, an hour had passed. There was definitely chemistry but also something else I couldn't quite pinpoint.

As the band began to play "Tennessee Waltz," John leaned over and asked, "Would you like to dance?" I gave him my hand, and a delicious shiver ran down my spine as he led me to the dance floor. He was an excellent dancer, almost better than dear Cary in my dreams. He also had wandering hands, it appeared. After I politely returned them to where they should have been, they didn't wander again...much.

Kathy had turned into the belle of the ball. She gave me a little wave and a huge smile as she twirled by with yet another partner. I closed my eyes and followed John's lead. All of a sudden he stopped at a tap on his shoulder.

"May I cut in?"

My eyes jerked open at the sound of Steve's voice. *Please let me be imagining things*, I thought as I turned around. Although what would that mean if I were? But there he was in the flesh—and a tuxedo. He didn't look pleased.

"What are you doing here?" I asked with hands on hips.

"I mentioned to your mother that I was going to be in Chicago this week, and she suggested I surprise you." He gave John a scathing glance. "It seems I did."

I made yet another mental note to self: never tell Mother anything about my plans in future. "Yes, this is a surprise." Even I could hear the edge in my voice.

John coughed slightly beside me.

"John Delancey, meet Steve Taylor. Steve's an old college friend of my brother's." I smiled sweetly as Steve's eyes narrowed.

"I'm a little more than that, Emma."

"Would you excuse us for a minute, John?" I grabbed Steve's arm and stalked off with him, leaving John in the middle of the floor. "Steve, you have the worst timing of anybody I know," I hissed. "Why are you here?"

"Emma, I've tried to see you all week, but you always had something else to do. When your mother told me you'd be here, I thought it would be nice for us to spend some time together."

"You couldn't have called me first?"

"I thought it would be a nice surprise, but obviously not." He looked hurt.

I was seriously beginning to hate surprises. "I'm sorry I was short, but please do not follow Mother's suggestions in future. Why are you in Chicago anyway?"

"I'm prepping a client for a deposition next week."

A little bell rang as the founder of the organization stepped to the podium. I turned back to Steve. "Look, the dinner is about to start. I've got to go."

"Why can't I stay?" he whined.

"Because it's an invitation-only event, Steve, and there's not a place for you at the table."

"Fine. Enjoy your evening," he said sarcastically. "Spinsterhood, yeah right," he mumbled as he walked away.

I hurried back to the table where Kathy was catching her breath. "Whew! My feet are killing me, but it sure is fun." Then she frowned. "What was *he* doing here?"

"Mother." That was all the explanation Kathy needed.

"Is everything all right?" John asked, seating himself.

"Wonderful, now. How's the lamb?"

"Delicious." And it was.

The rest of the evening flew by in a blur of farewell speeches and dancing. John walked us to the elevator that would take Kathy and me to our rooms. "Kathy, it was lovely meeting you," he said. The elevator doors opened, and she stepped inside. "Emma, I'd really like to see you again."

He trailed his hand down my arm, and the skin tingled where he touched it in a slightly unpleasant way like the hairs standing on the back of your neck when you feel you're being watched. From our conversations, I had gotten the impression that he wasn't all he seemed, but I was probably just being paranoid.

"I'm going to be in Dallas in a few weeks," he continued. "Could we get together then?" I hesitated, and he added, "To discuss business, of course."

I wasn't sure about him, but his connection to collectors could be invaluable. I decided to ignore my nagging suspicion. "I'd love to." I handed him one of my cards. "Call me," I said as I joined Kathy in the elevator.

"I will," he said, smiling speculatively.

The elevator doors closed, and Kathy and I started giggling like schoolgirls. "What a hunk!" she exclaimed, fanning herself vigorously with her hand.

"You're not kidding, and he dances like a dream." I melted against the side of the elevator then frowned. "Except for the wandering hands, that is."

"I hate when men do that. You should have seen Steve's face when he spotted the two of you together. I thought he would have an aneurysm for sure."

I rolled my eyes. "I could kill Mother. She's like a pit bull; once she gets hold of an idea, she just won't let go."

"Honey, that woman was born to push everybody around."

I fully agreed with her. "Don't I know it!" Deciding it was time to change the subject, I said, "You sure seemed to be enjoying yourself this evening."

Her blue eyes sparkled. "What fun! I haven't danced this much in years."

"Who was the guy dressed like the ringmaster? He looked absolutely dazzled by you." That sent us into another fit of giggles. The elevator doors opened about that time, and the people waiting to get on looked at us like we'd lost our minds.

"Oh," Kathy gasped for breath, attempting to answer my question. "That was Donnie. What a teddy bear! He's a buyer for one of the larger bookstores. Can you believe he's just down the road from us in Irving?"

"And?" I asked.

"And I got his number," she replied, looking like the cat that ate the canary.

I pretended to be shocked. "How liberated of you!"

"I know."

"Are you going to call him?"

"You can bet your bottom I am, but not until Monday. Wouldn't want him to think I was desperate or anything."

I shook my head in admiration. "There's no way he could think you were desperate after tonight. The men were lined up waiting to dance with you."

Kathy wiggled her eyebrows mischievously. "But absence makes the heart grow fonder, as they always say, so I'll give him the weekend to dream about me."

We were still laughing as we went to our rooms.

Chapter Seven

BRIAN WAS WAITING on my doorstep when Kathy pulled into my drive.

"What a nice surprise!" I exclaimed, still in the car. I had to admit that I felt a little giddy in that moment. My heart was pounding and I felt flushed.

"Take another look, honey. He doesn't look happy," Kathy cautioned. I looked out the window and saw that he was pacing.

"What could possibly have happened now?" I sighed as my bubble of happiness deflated.

"You better go see what he wants before he wears a path in the concrete."

As I ascended the porch steps, Brian exploded, "Your dog bit me!"

"Well, I missed you too," I said coldly. "What happened?"

He relaxed slightly. "Sorry, I'm just a little upset. He's in the backyard, by the way. After Delilah and I had dinner last night, we came back to my place to watch a movie. I let Mike into the house, and everything was fine until she got ready to leave. I was giving her a hug when your dog charged up behind me growling and bit me in the rear."

I couldn't help it; I burst out laughing at the image of Mike with a mouthful of Brian's backside. "I'm sorry," I said, trying to straighten my face.

He frowned. "It's not funny."

"You're right; it's not funny."

He was dead serious, and then I realized something else. He had not been "hugging" Delilah. I stopped laughing. "You were kissing her, weren't you?"

"Well, uh, I..." He looked extremely uncomfortable.

"Forget it. Doesn't matter to me," I said nonchalantly and unlocked the door. "You won't have to worry about Mike biting you anymore. I'll find a boarding kennel next time." I stepped inside.

"Emma, wait. I didn't mean—"

I cut him off with a "Good night," and shut the door. Leaving my luggage in the entryway, I grabbed the dog treats and a pint of chocolate ice cream on the way to let Michelangelo in from the backyard. I put the ice cream and treats on the bedside table, stripped to my undies, put Keith Urban in the CD player, and plopped into bed.

"Come on, Mike." I patted the bed. He put one foot on the coverlet and eyed me warily. I didn't usually let him sleep with me, and he wasn't sure I meant it now. I grabbed the treats and rattled the bag. "Come on, boy." He bounded onto the bed and lay down by my side. I gave him a handful of dog treats and scratched his ears. "Good boy, Mike." I knew it was irrational to reward him for his behavior, but I was in no mood to do otherwise.

I grabbed my pint of ice cream and munched away while listening to Keith sing "You'll Think of Me." I've always believed there is a Keith Urban song for every occasion or emotion. I was halfway through the pint when the phone rang.

"Did you get my present?" Mother asked, a mischievous tone in her voice, skipping the lecture for once.

"Yes, I did." I stabbed my spoon into the ice cream. "Please don't send any more like it."

She was immediately affronted. "Well, forgive me, Miss High-and-Mighty. I just thought since you were both in the same city, it might be nice if you could have dinner together."

I sighed in exasperation. "Mother, the point is that I already had plans, and I was already having dinner with someone."

"Who?" Dang it!

"Kathy, of course." I tried to sound nonchalant, but evidently it wasn't working.

"It wouldn't have bothered you so much if you were just with Kathy. Who is he?" she demanded.

She'd never stop bugging me if I didn't answer her. "Well, there was a man with us."

"Who is he?"

I gave up. "His name is John Delancey, and he's from New York."

"New York!" The disappointment in her voice was loud and clear. "How are y'all supposed to get to know each other if you never see him?"

"Well, they do still have telephones, and I'm sure you've heard of a little thing called e-mail," I answered sarcastically.

"Very funny, smarty pants."

"Besides, I'm not dating anymore, remember? He's strictly a business connection."

She chose to ignore that. "What does he do for a living?"

"He acts as middleman between buyers and sellers of collectibles. He travels a lot. In fact, he said he'll be in Texas in a few weeks."

"Am I going to get to meet him?"

No way was that going to happen. "We'll be meeting to discuss business only," I assured her.

"Do you think I'm so horrible that I'll scare him off?" she asked petulantly.

"No, Mother." *Maybe just a little*, I thought to myself. "This is just strictly business so there's no need for him to meet you."

She wasn't mollified. "I can't believe you're persisting in this ridiculous spinsterhood thing. You're never going to get a husband if you don't date, Emma."

"Which is exactly the point." I pinched the bridge of my nose between my fingers. Either she or the ice cream was giving me a headache. "I believe we've already had this conversation before, Mother." The phone beeped in my ear. Saved by the bell! "Someone's beeping in; I have to go."

"But, Emma—"

"Sorry. I'll talk to you later." I clicked over to the other line. "Hello?"

"Emma, I didn't mean that I didn't want to keep Mike anymore." It was Brian. "I was just venting, and you took it the wrong way."

I ate another mouthful of ice cream a little too fast. "Ow, crap!"

"What are you doing?"

I waited for the brain freeze to subside. "Eating ice cream."

"For dinner or dessert?"

He knew too much about me. "Dinner," I confessed.

"What flavor?"

"Chocolate, of course." At least he didn't know everything.

"Listen. I have kung pao chicken over here, and you have ice cream. Why don't I bring mine over, and we'll share?" he wheedled.

I stewed on that for a minute. "Fine, but bring it to the bedroom. I'm too lazy to get out of bed." I hung up and settled back against the pillows. Wait a minute! I was still in my bra and panties! I raced over to the dresser and pulled on a pair of pajamas, hearing the front door open as I jumped back into bed.

Brian stuck his head in the doorway. "Truce?"

Michelangelo growled and raised his head.

"I think you better ask him," I replied. Brian produced a new squeaky toy from behind his back and tossed it to the dog. Michelangelo caught it and wagged his tail. "I think you're forgiven. Mike, down." Michelangelo jumped off the bed and lay down on the floor beside me. I turned on the TV and started searching for a movie to watch.

Keith had switched to "Making Memories of Us" as Brian kicked off his shoes and sweatshirt, which he'd worn over a George Strait T-shirt, then sat down on the other side of the bed and pulled Chinese takeout cartons from a bag. "I just had it delivered, so it's still warm." He passed the kung pao and started on the fried rice. After a few bites, we switched cartons.

"So how was the rest of your evening before the dog biting incident?" I asked.

"It was great," he said around a mouthful of chicken. "I really think you'd like her."

I just nodded my head and kept eating. *I wouldn't count on it, buddy.*

He broke the silence. "So how was the convention?"

"Busy, but fabulous." I swallowed before adding, "I met a very nice man there."

"Oh?" A fleeting frown crossed his face.

"His name's John Delancey, and he deals in collectibles. He's actually going to be in Texas in a few weeks, and we're going to have dinner." He looked disappointed. "To discuss business," I added.

His face cheered right up. "That's nice. So what are we watching?"

"*Gone with the Wind.*"

"'Frankly, my dear...' What a great line. Pass the ice cream." I did. "Hey! You ate it all!"

"I did not," I protested. "There's still some in the bottom."

"Huh. Two bites maybe," he muttered.

"Quit your whining and finish it." I took the empty cartons to the trash and jumped back into bed, tossing Brian around on the other side.

"Didn't your mother ever teach you not to jump on beds?" he complained.

I smacked him with a pillow, which he kept with a smirk. I stuck my tongue out at him and lay back down, switching the music off. We both fell silent as we watched Scarlett trying to get her man, whomever it happened to be at the moment. Boy, did that sound familiar.

I was lying in Cary Grant's arms, and I felt so secure. I could feel his breath on my neck and his chest firm against my back. I snuggled closer and pulled his arms tighter around me. His face faded and came back into focus, but it wasn't Cary's face at all. It was Brian's. I rested my hand against his face and whispered, "I love you."

My eyes flew open. My heart was pounding. *Just a dream*, I thought, and my pulse slowed down a little. It charged back again when I looked down and noticed I really was wrapped in someone's arms. Not just someone's arms; they really did belong to Brian! I rolled over quietly, trying not to wake him.

Even up close, I had to admit he was gorgeous. His lashes were thick against his cheeks. His nose was a little crooked on the end from a fistfight in his younger years. His lips were full and nicely shaped. Gazing at this face that I had seen every day for so long, I knew at that moment that I did love him, and not just as a friend.

The epiphany was devastating. I was in love with this man, a man I knew did not share my feelings. Worse, he was my best friend, so I couldn't talk to him about it. Plus I had already declared I never wanted to get married—with him as a witness!

My hand flew to my mouth as he opened one eye blearily and smiled. Why had I never noticed how beautiful his smile was before? I thought my heart was going to break in two at the sight of it.

"Good morning, sunshine," he said as he gave me a big hug. I couldn't speak for fear of blurting everything out to him. "I guess we fell asleep, huh?" I just nodded. "What's the matter? Cat got your tongue?"

I had to say something, or I was going to look like the fool I felt. "Uh, I just need to brush my teeth. You know, morning breath and all." I giggled nervously. *Oh God, please don't let me get hysterical,* I prayed silently.

He looked at me curiously. "What time is it?"

I turned over and glanced at the clock. "Ten o'clock." I just realized I had not woken at six as I normally did. My entire body was turning mutinous. "We should get up."

"Nonsense. It's Saturday," he said and pulled me back against him. I was sure he could feel my heart pounding at the touch of his arms just below my breasts. I had to get out of here.

The digital lights of the clock flashed before my eyes again. I sat up quickly and scrambled off the bed. "Brian! It's not Saturday! It's Sunday! We're going to be late for church!" I could just see the look on my mother's face if we walked in late together.

"Crap! I've got to go pick up Delilah." He sat up and started pulling on his shoes. "I'll meet you there."

I stopped dead in my run for the bathroom, or tried, at least; socks and hardwood floors tend to make that impossible. After tripping all over myself to stay upright, I looked at him in disbelief. "You're bringing her to church?"

"Yeah. She wanted to meet you, so I invited her." He stood up and headed for the door.

"Oh, okay. See you there then." I heard the front door close behind him. I would have to meet her on a day when I didn't have much time to get ready. I flew to the bathroom and brushed my teeth. Now what to wear? I had to look good. I grabbed my favorite blue dress, which showed off my figure while being conservative enough for church. It just happened to be Brian's favorite too.

I ran back to the mirror and looked at the disaster that was my hair. I didn't have time to wash and style it, so I threw it up into a French twist. *Not bad*, I thought, carefully applying my makeup to bring out my eyes. I had always thought they were my best feature. I added the lip gloss Brian had liked for good measure.

I put Michelangelo in the backyard a little grouchily. Any other morning he would have been licking my face to wake me up long before now. *If I didn't know any better, I'd think the universe was conspiring against me*, I thought wryly.

I locked up, got in my car, and sped to the church. Trotting up the front steps, I looked at my watch: five minutes to spare. I took a minute to catch my breath before opening the door. Anne and Teddy were already there.

She turned to say good morning.

"Oh, Anne." I could feel my eyes welling. *Please, God, I can't cry today. Please help me stay in control.*

She grabbed my hands. "Emma, you're trembling," she whispered. "What's wrong?"

"Hello, everyone," I heard Brian say behind me, but I couldn't turn around yet. I needed another second.

Anne looked over my shoulder at him, and then back at my crestfallen face. She gave my hands a powerful clasp and stepped around me. "Good morning, Brian." I took a few more breaths, said another little prayer, and turned around.

Brian had a big smile on his face. "Everyone, this is Delilah. Delilah, this is Anne and Teddy Bailey." Then he turned to me. "And this is Emma."

As we looked at each other, both of us recognized each other for what we were: rivals. She wasn't the raven-haired, violet-eyed seductress I had imagined. She was a stylishly coiffed, blonde-haired seductress with eyes so blue I knew they had to be contact lenses. *Score one for me*, I thought. I was all natural, and she obviously wasn't in more ways than one.

"Emma, it's so nice to meet you," she said sweetly, shaking my hand. Her grip left no doubt that war had been declared. "I've heard so much about you."

Thankfully I didn't have to reply; at that moment, Steve stepped over and put his arm around me. "How's my lady today?"

I shrugged away his arm. "I'm not your lady." I glanced over at Brian, but he only had eyes for "Barbie." I decided to try things a little differently, and Steve was readily available.

"I do hope you're staying for dinner, Steve," I said coyly. Out of the corner of my eye, I saw Brian's head snap around. That had gotten his attention. Steve looked stunned.

There was that slow smile again. "Absolutely."

"I seem to have forgotten my manners," I said in mock embarrassment. "Steve, this is Brian's friend, Delilah. Delilah, this is Steve Taylor."

The organist began to play an opening hymn, so we turned to file into the pew. I came face to face with Mother, who looked ecstatic, and Anne, who was frowning with concern. I lifted my chin, smiled, and moved past them to sit down. Steve settled his arm around me on the back of the pew as Brian and Delilah filed past to sit beside us. I could have strangled her when she rested her hand possessively on his knee.

I spent the entire sermon watching them unobtrusively while fending off Steve's hands and trying to understand

Brian's apparent fascination with her. He had never gone for the Barbie type before, and it was unsettling. I was completely out of sorts. Maybe I didn't know him as well as I thought I did.

After church, Mother was delayed by several of her friends, but it didn't take long for her to come over to where we were standing. "Brian, I insist that you and Delilah stay for dinner with us. We'd be delighted to have you."

I held my breath praying that they'd say no.

"Is that all right with you, Delilah?" Brian asked. He was holding her hand, I noticed.

She looked at me and smiled smugly. "I'd love it."

Dinner was a nightmare. I spent the entire time trying to ignore Brian and Delilah as they whispered together as well as Steve's increasing attentions. I was also trying to avoid the looks I was getting from the rest of my family.

"So, Emma." Delilah finally spoke up from the other side of the table. "Brian tells me that you own a bookstore."

"That's right." I smiled sweetly back at her.

"What kind of books do you sell?" she asked, feigning interest.

"Children's books." Brian was watching the interplay between us carefully.

"Not any kind of *real* literature?" she asked, not quite managing to keep the disdain from her voice. Anne nearly choked on her tea, but I kept silent. "Oh. Well, I'm sure you must really enjoy it," she said, as if highly doubting that anyone could.

"Yes, I do, and there's actually a lot of money involved in children's books. In fact, I have one book that's worth fifty thousand dollars alone." I smiled innocently, knowing that the amount was more than her annual salary at the junior college. Brian frowned slightly, and I almost felt ashamed for bragging. Almost.

Her smile faltered a second. "Well, money isn't everything."

"You're quite right, which is exactly why I haven't sold it, although I've had many offers." I looked at my dad and continued. "It has more value to me than money." It was his sister who had given me the books. Dad reached over and gave my hand a quick squeeze.

Obviously uncomfortable, Delilah turned back to Brian and whispered in his ear. "If everyone will excuse us," he said as they rose from the table, "Delilah just reminded me of a party that we've been invited to this evening, so I'm afraid we must be going. Mrs. Bailey, your cooking was delicious as always."

"Actually, I have to be going too," Steve spoke up. "Mr. and Mrs. Bailey, thank you for having me again. Emma, walk me to the door?"

"Sure." I followed him down the hall to the door as Brian and Delilah finished saying their good-byes.

"Can I assume that your actions today mean I've been forgiven?" he asked.

"Well, let's just say you're on probation—as a friend, of course." My conscience was beginning to prick me for using him.

"I'll take this kind of probation anytime." He ignored the friend comment and gave me a peck on the cheek as Brian and Delilah reached the end of the hall. "Call you later?" he whispered.

I nodded distractedly and stepped aside to let Brian and Delilah get to the door as he turned and left. "Emma, it was a pleasure to meet you," she said with her mouth, but her eyes made it clear that it hadn't been.

"You too. Y'all have fun at the party," I said as she stepped through the door. Then I turned to face Brian.

"What was that all about?" he asked, staring at Steve's retreating figure.

"What do you mean?" I asked innocently.

"I thought you weren't dating." The disgust was evident on his face.

"I'm not dating." I folded my arms and looked him squarely in the eye. "I was politely saying good-bye to a friend."

"Steve's your friend now?" he asked in disbelief.

"Why not? I've put the past solidly behind me and moved on. I can handle it." Something flickered in his eyes, but he remained silent. He didn't believe me. "You don't think I can, do you?" He still didn't say anything, but he was beginning to look uncomfortable. I had just realized how he must have been seeing me all this time. "You think I'm just some pathetic, wimpy woman who's easily duped, don't you?" I asked quietly. I turned as my eyes welled once again, and I left him silent at the door.

❧

"So," Mother said as I entered the kitchen after composing myself. "You and Steve looked awfully cozy together. Have y'all decided to start dating again?" She was washing dishes, and Anne was drying them. Mother didn't trust the dish-

washer to truly get the dishes clean, as if reusing dirty water
was going to get the job done better.

"No," I said a little too adamantly. "Let's just say we're testing the waters of friendship." Anne looked at me dubiously.

Mother tried hard to keep the excitement out of her
voice. "That's always a good first step."

"Don't start planning any wedding, Mother. This isn't a
first step toward anything."

Anne dried the last dish and followed me down the hall.
"Okay, Emma, what is going on here?"

"I don't want to talk about it here," I said in a low voice.
"Let's go to my house."

She nodded. "I'll just tell Teddy to pick me up after
they've finished watching the game."

❧

We settled on the couch in my living room with cups of tea.
Being from the South, where iced sweet tea was the drink of
choice, our family could never understand how Anne and
I drank our tea hot, but we preferred it that way no matter what time of the year it was. It was a little quirk we'd
discovered we had in common that first evening Teddy had
brought her home to meet the family.

"There's nothing as relaxing as a cup of great tea with a
friend." She sighed contentedly. "Now tell me what's wrong."

I shook my head. "Not yet. Tell me about your honeymoon first. We didn't really have a chance to talk about it," I
added, remembering their first Sunday back and the dinner
afterward.

"Well, we didn't leave the room much," she started
teasingly.

"Yuck!" I pretended to gag. "Too much information. Please remember that Teddy is my brother," I said and laughed.

"No, really, the Bahamas were wonderful." She continued to tell me all about the diving they had done and all the great food they had eaten.

"I hope y'all took pictures, and I mean outside of the hotel room."

Anne was an avid photographer. She chuckled. "I think I filled up three memory cards. Now before I die of suspense, please tell me what I missed this week."

I took a deep breath and plunged in. The words poured out about Steve, my palpitations around Brian, and his growing involvement with Delilah. "Then, this morning, when I woke up with Brian's arms around me, I knew that I loved him, had loved him for a while without knowing it. It was awful," I moaned as I threw my head back against the couch.

Anne's brow wrinkled. "Why was it awful?"

"Because I've declared myself an old maid, and he doesn't feel the same way about me. You saw the way he drooled over that...that...Delilah this morning." It was better to just say her name. I took a sip of tea to cleanse the taste of it from my mouth. The name was descriptive enough and far cleaner than the words I had been thinking of using.

She placed a hand on my arm. "Emma, your declaration was just words. You didn't sign a contract or anything. You're allowed to change how you feel." Anne asked gently, "Are you going to tell him?"

I leaned forward to set my teacup on the coffee table and shook my head. "I can't. If I tell him, he'll take all the blame and withdraw from me so he won't hurt me. Besides, he was so proud of me for being strong and standing up for myself, or at least I thought he was." I straightened and lifted my chin. "I'll just have to hide how I feel and try to move on with my life. I can do that if I can just see him and talk to him." My bravado fell with my shoulders as I shook my head and whispered in anguish, "I just can't lose him, Anne."

I felt her hand on my chin as she turned my face to hers. "Is that why you played up to Steve today?"

I dropped my eyes. "Yes. I know it was stupid." I stood and walked to the window with my arms wrapped around my waist trying to stave off the chill around my heart. "I couldn't let anybody see that Brian's bringing a woman to church had upset me. I'd be 'Poor Emma' forever, and I can stand anything but that."

Anne had followed me and now placed her own arms around me and rested her chin on my shoulder, trying to give me comfort. "I'm so sorry, Emma. I wish I could just wave a wand and make Brian love you so that you could be as happy as I am."

I leaned my head against hers while blinking away my tears. "I'm sorry to dump all this on you. It's seems like all I do is whine to you, and I'm turning into a weepy woman, which I absolutely hate."

She gave me one last hug and went back to her tea. "It happens to the best of us. If you try to hold it all in, you're going to blow up at some point."

I followed and retrieved my own cup with a grim smile. "That's a chance I'll have to take."

Our discussion moved on, and soon Teddy arrived to take his wife home. I let Michelangelo in for his supper and company. "Looks like it's just you and me tonight, buddy." I grabbed another pint of chocolate ice cream and headed for the bedroom to see what was on Turner Classic Movies.

"*Casablanca*. Perfect," I said sarcastically. "Good old Bogey leaves Ingrid for her own good. That's exactly what Brian would do if I told him. Great, now I'm talking to myself. Pretty soon I'll be ready for a straitjacket."

Attempting to clean up some of the mess around my room, I noticed something lying on the floor by the side of the bed. It was Brian's sweatshirt. I picked it up and held it to my face, inhaling deeply. It smelled just like him and his cologne. Without even thinking, I slipped it over my head and climbed in bed. I grabbed the pint and dug in.

The phone rang. "Hello," I answered around a mouthful of ice cream.

"Emma? Is this Emma Bailey?"

I sat up and swallowed. "This is she."

"It's John Delancey from New York."

I'd forgotten all about him. "How are you?"

"I'm fine, and you?"

"Great." Not really, but I couldn't very well tell him that.

"I wanted to call and tell you what a wonderful time I had talking to you on Friday evening."

"Thank you; I enjoyed talking to you as well," I added politely.

"Listen, I'm going to be in town on the weekend of October twenty-first, and I was wondering if we could get together for dinner. I'd really like to see you again and discuss some business."

"Just a sec." I ran to get my Blackberry out of my purse and checked my calendar. *This is stupid. It's not like your dance card is filled or anything.* "That would be great. Why don't you just call me when you get to town, and we'll meet somewhere?"

"Wonderful. I'll see you then. Good night."

"Okay, good night." I sat back against the pillows and finished my ice cream thoughtfully. Maybe if I kept my mind busy with work, my feelings for Brian would just fade away. Probably wishful thinking on my part, but it was worth a try. Michelangelo rested his head in my lap again.

The phone rang again. "How's my girl tonight?" Steve. I had forgotten that he'd said he was going to call. Well, at least he was a man of his word—so far.

"I'm not your girl, Steve," I said for what felt like the millionth time.

"I was calling to see if you'd have dinner with me this Saturday, just as friends."

I didn't bother checking my calendar again. I knew it was blank. "Sounds good. What did you have in mind?" I knew I'd probably regret it, but at this point, I just didn't care anymore.

"Just leave the planning to me, but we'll need to eat an early dinner. Pick you up at five?"

"I'll see you then."

"Great! Sweet dreams."

"'Night." *All right*, I thought. Two weekends planned in one night. So far, the distractions were supplying themselves. *Let's hope this keeps up.*

I turned back to the TV and decided that I didn't want to see Bogey leave Bergman again. I turned it off and snuggled under the covers with my nose in Brian's sweatshirt. Sleep eluded me as the day's events kept replaying through my mind. I didn't want to keep my mind occupied. I only wanted Brian.

Chapter Eight

I FINALLY SLEPT, although not well, but at least my internal alarm clock was working again the next morning. I stayed in bed hoping to make up a little of the sleep I'd lost during the night, but it wasn't working. My thoughts from the previous night were insistently looping through my brain, causing all chance of dozing to be lost. I'd crawled out of bed and just started coffee when the doorbell rang, and I hurried to answer it after letting Michelangelo out into the backyard. Brian was standing there with dog toy in hand.

It felt like a knife went right through my heart. He looked so good with the sun glinting in his hair and that smile that caused my heart to do a little flip. "I found one of Mike's toys and thought he might be missing it." He handed it to me and looked at me curiously.

"What?" I asked, throwing my hands to my hair.

"You're wearing my sweatshirt."

"I am?" I looked down. Oh God, I was. I could feel the redness creeping up my neck. *Play it cool, Emma.* "Sorry. I just grabbed something off the floor when the doorbell rang. I didn't realize it was yours; I'll get it back to you."

"No problem."

I turned and started back to the kitchen, cringing at the thought of the way we left things yesterday. "Want some coffee?" I asked.

"Sure."

I handed him a cup and sat at the bar. He was absently staring at the cup in his hand.

"So what brings you over this morning, neighbor?" I asked, wanting to get this over with as soon as possible. I kept my eyes on my own cup.

He sat on the stool next to me and pushed the cup away from my hands before turning my stool so I had to face him. He looked so serious. I didn't realize I'd been fidgeting until he took my hands to make me stop.

"Emma, I've never thought you were pathetic." His thumbs caressed the backs of my hands. He had such strong, capable hands that could also be so gentle. I just wanted to hide my face in them, but he was talking again. "When I first met you, you definitely were not very confident. You were wounded, but you were never a wimp."

He reached up and cupped my face. "You've changed so much in the last few months," he whispered and looked at me in such a way as he never had before that I started to panic about what he was going to say next. I was trying to think of something to do to keep him from speaking again, but my mind had drawn a complete blank. "Emma, what I'm trying to say is—"

"It's okay, Brian," I interrupted. "You don't have to say anything. I overreacted yesterday. I'm sorry." I took our coffee cups to the sink. I glanced at the clock and saw that it was nearly eight. "You should get on the road if you're going to be at work by nine," I added.

He looked disappointed as he glanced at his watch. "I'll see you later then," he called back before closing the door behind him.

"Be safe," I whispered to myself.

"So did you have a good weekend?" I was asking Kathy an hour later when I arrived at work.

"Actually, I did." She was practically beaming. "Donnie called me yesterday."

"I told you he couldn't resist your charms. So what'd you talk about?"

"Oh, this and that. You know what the first few conversations are like. We did make plans to go out this weekend."

"Good, I'm glad to hear it."

"What about you? How was *your* weekend?"

I stopped arranging books for a minute, thinking about Brian for about the hundredth time. My face must have shown how crestfallen I felt, because Kathy stepped closer and asked, "What's happened?"

I told her all about my Sunday morning bombshell. "I can't believe I've let myself fall in love with someone who doesn't share my feelings *again*," I said, wiping my eyes with a tissue Kathy had produced from the desk.

"Are you sure he doesn't?" she asked quietly.

"Yes." I told her about his bringing Delilah to church so she could meet everyone. "She's so fake, and she tried every way in the world to make me look bad. Brian was just oblivious. I can't believe he's so moony-eyed over her."

"Oh, honey. I'm so sorry." She put her arm around my shoulders and gave me a hug.

I squared my shoulders. "It doesn't matter. If I can keep myself busy like with the dinner this weekend, then I can just continue being Brian's friend and live my life."

She didn't look like she believed me, but for the moment she had the courtesy not to tell me so. "What's this about a dinner this weekend?"

"I'm having dinner with Steve," I said, quickly rearranging more books just to have something to do so as not to meet her eyes.

"Oh, dear. Are you sure that's a good idea?"

"Not now that I've thought about it, but I was so upset when he asked I just accepted. Crap!"

"What is it?"

"I forgot John called last night before I thought any of this over. He'll be down in a few weeks, and I'm supposed to have dinner with him." I added grimly, "I'll just have to make it clear that it's a business relationship only." I didn't think I could take much more drama.

The bell jingled, announcing the first customers of the morning. It was a nonstop flow after that and for the rest of the week. I went home exhausted every night, wondering what in the world inspired me to have this sale every year and upset that I hadn't heard from Brian. I just knew he was spending all of that time with Delilah. I was already losing my best friend to that woman.

❦

Steve had called several times that week to chat and drop hints about the evening he had planned for Saturday. "Wear that green dress you had on at the convention. It'll be perfect." I couldn't believe he had remembered that I was wearing a dress, much less the color. He'd never noticed anything like that in past, at least not on me. Maybe he *had* changed.

I had also had a few e-mails from John. He kept asking questions about my Nancy Drew books and if he could see them when he was in town. He also kept relaying offers for them from prospective buyers. I kept rejecting them as politely as possible.

Saturday evening finally rolled around, and I donned the green dress as requested. I was putting a last coat of gloss over my lipstick when the doorbell rang. I opened it expecting Steve but found Brian standing there instead. I really had to get a peephole installed. I wasn't sure my heart could take many more surprise visits, and unfortunately none of my front windows offered a view of the entryway.

"Wow," he whistled as I invited him inside. "You look spectacular."

"Thanks," I responded dully.

He seemed oblivious. "What's the occasion?"

"I'm going out to dinner." I started back toward the bedroom to finish getting ready.

He followed. "Really? I was hoping we could do something tonight since we haven't seen each other all week."

"Well, I've been here all week." I was terse because he just expected I'd be sitting at home on a Saturday night—and because it was usually the truth.

My tone had made him bristle a little. "Well, I was working a lot of hours this week trying to implement the new data management system at the bank, and I was with Delilah last night."

"And where is she tonight?" I called from the closet as I searched for my heels.

"She went to a birthday party for her dad."

"I see." I stuck my head out. "So because your girlfriend wasn't available, you decided you'd spend time with your good old standby. Sorry, but the standby has plans. I'm sure Mike would be delighted to sit with you."

He was looking at me like I was a complete stranger. Then his expression started to darken. "That's not why I came over here at all."

The doorbell rang again, and this time it was Steve. He looked great in his black suit and a green tie that matched the color of my dress exactly. *Wow, good memory*, I thought. Looking at the two of them facing each other in the entryway, I was beginning to have an unpleasant déjà vu moment.

"Ready?" Steve asked.

"You're going out with *him*?" Distaste was evident on Brian's face.

"I'm *having dinner* with him," I emphasized as Steve placed my wrap around my shoulders. "I believe you can show yourself out." I led Steve out, leaving Brian standing in the doorway.

I looked back at him once I was seated in the car. His face was shadowed, his features unreadable, but every line of his body conveyed anger. I wanted to run back to him and start the whole evening over, but it was too late. Me and my big mouth. I had been hurt, so I had intentionally set out to do the same to him. I didn't deserve him, and I closed my eyes against the tears as Steve pulled out of the drive.

Luckily I had regained my composure by the time we arrived at Swan Court for dinner. The veal picatta was wonderful, as was the peach sorbet. After the waiter cleared our plates from the table, Steve reached to take my hand. "Feeling better?" he asked.

"Am I that transparent?" I pulled my hand away and settled it in my lap far from his reach. "It's been a long week." His concern was an improvement from previous experiences, but I wasn't about to tell him the real reason for my being upset. "So what's this big surprise you've been hinting about all week?"

"I'm taking you to the opera."

I was a huge fan of the opera, but he wasn't. "You hate the opera!" I exclaimed.

"I don't hate it. I just had to develop an appreciation for it." The waiter had brought our bill, and Steve handed him enough cash to cover it plus a generous tip.

"You're humoring me, but I don't care. What's playing?" I asked excitedly.

"*The Barber of Seville*."

"You're kidding." It was my favorite and had been ever since I had seen it as "The Rabbit of Seville" on Bugs Bunny when I was much younger. I felt a little pang as I remembered that this was Brian's favorite cartoon as well as mine. I shrugged it off.

Steve was grinning. "No, I'm not, and we have great seats. In fact, we should be going," he said, helping me out of my seat.

Sure enough, we were in the middle section at the Music Hall, only a few rows back from the orchestra pit. "Steve, these seats are perfect. They must have cost a fortune!"

"I spare no expense for my lady."

I bristled at the possessive term, but had no chance to say anything as he asked, "Would you like something to drink?"

"No, thank you. I'm fine."

He sat beside me and took my hand in his. I pulled it away and opened my program. We talked quietly before the lights lowered, announcing the beginning of the first act. I sat enthralled from the very beginning. The music was wonderful, and the vocalists could not have been better.

We rose from our seats as the curtain fell, shouting "Bravo!" and clapping wildly. He took my arm as we left the theater and waited at the valet stand for his car to be brought around. On the way home, we discussed the opera and then turned to other subjects such as work and family. I was pleasantly surprised because it seemed he might have actually done some growing up.

He walked me to the door but didn't follow me inside. "Would you like to come in?" I asked politely and walked back to the doorway.

"Emma," he said softly, taking my hand. "If I come in, I'm not going to want to leave." His eyes begged me to ask him in again.

I shook my head. "I'm sorry, Steve, I just..." My voice trailed off at the disappointment on his face. "I'll see you at church tomorrow?"

Before I knew it, he had pulled me close and leaned down, stopping just before our lips met. "I'll be there." His breath was warm on my lips, and for one moment I allowed myself to melt into oblivion and forget everything as he pulled me closer and kissed me hungrily. I felt his hands trail up my spine and into my hair with a flare of warmth trailing behind. My body was responding, but my mind had rebelled. An image of Brian's face flickered for an instant across my mind, and I pulled away, pushing against him with my hands to put some distance between us.

"We shouldn't have done that," I whispered somewhat out of breath.

He took my hands in his from where they lay against his chest and kissed the palm of each one before looking at me with a crooked grin. "Why not?"

"Because I don't love you," I blurted.

He smiled slowly. "That's not what it felt like to me."

My face burned in shame as I pushed away from him. "I'm sorry, but it's true. Good night, Steve." I held open the door.

He wiped my gloss from his lips and smiled again smugly. "Sweet dreams, Emma." He walked to his car, smoothing his hair and straightening his tie.

I shut the door and paced in the entryway, willing my heart to quit pounding and my body to quit feeling like a string wound too tightly and ready to break. I didn't think being friends with Steve was going to work. I went to the back door, thinking a game of fetch with Michelangelo might soothe my nerves, but he didn't answer my call, and he was nowhere to be found. My heart raced again, but this time it was fear. Where was he? Had he gotten out somehow and ran away? Had he been stolen?

I ran back into the house and grabbed for the phone with only one thought in mind. Call Brian. That's when I saw the note stuck to the refrigerator door. It read, "Emma, I took you up on your offer to have Mike sit with me tonight. You'll find him at my place when you get back." I was so relieved to know that Michelangelo wasn't gone that I ran straight to Brian's and knocked on the door.

"Don't ever take my dog like that again," I greeted him as I burst inside. "You almost scared me to death."

"I left a note on the refrigerator because I figured you'd head straight for the chocolate ice cream after your date with Steve," he said sarcastically. "Obviously it went better than I had anticipated."

I threw my hands on my hips in outrage. "It wasn't a date, and just what do you mean by that?"

He smirked. "Well, for starters, your lipstick is smeared, and your hair looks like a rat's nest."

I threw my hands up to cover my trembling mouth as embarrassment and shame coursed over me. I had been so scared about Michelangelo that I hadn't taken any time to change out of my dress, much less check my appearance; now Brian knew that I had been kissing Steve. Tears sprang to my eyes, and I tried not to blink so that they wouldn't fall.

"Hey, Emma," he said and grabbed my shoulders. He looked at me with concern. "I was only teasing. I don't care who you kiss." He took me in his arms, not knowing that he'd just made the pain twice as hard to bear. He didn't care. It kept repeating in my brain over and over.

I stepped away from him and lifted my chin, looking him squarely in the eye. "It was a mistake, which I made clear to Steve tonight."

Again he looked at me as if seeing me for the first time. "You don't have to explain anything; it's really none of my business. I'm sorry about earlier. I should have called you and asked about your plans before just showing up on your doorstep. I guess it just became a habit to assume that you would be free because you had been for so long."

Nothing like kicking a girl when she's down, I thought. "Can I have my dog back now?" I asked coldly.

Brian reached a hand behind his head and rubbed his neck wearily. "I'm sorry, Emma. That didn't come out right. I'm screwing this up royally." He retrieved Mike from the bedroom, and I took his leash in my hand.

"Don't worry about it. I'll see you tomorrow."

"Actually, I'm going to visit Delilah's church tomorrow."

"Oh." Numbness had kicked in by this point. "Okay, well, I'll talk to you later then. Come on, Mike."

I walked back to the house and fell into bed, pulling the covers over my head, green satin dress and all.

❦

I was lying in bed full of dread at having to see Steve at church in just a few hours. The telephone rang and interrupted my musings. Only Mother would dare call me this early. Everybody else knew I was not a morning person even if I was an early riser. "Hello, Mother," I said groggily.

"Well, did you and Steve work things out last night?"

"Mother, it's going to take more than dinner and an opera to make things better."

"Now, Emma. Steve's a nice young man, and ya'll were so happy together. Give him another chance. Neither of you are getting any younger, and that biological clock must be ticking. If you're going to give me grandchildren, you better get started quickly."

"Mother, my whole life doesn't have to revolve around giving you grandchildren. I'm quite happy being single." I was beginning to think about changing my phone number and conveniently forgetting to tell her, but then I realized that she'd only show up on my doorstep. Better to have her out of reach so I couldn't strangle her. "Besides, Teddy and Anne are married now. Shouldn't you be talking to them about grandchildren? At least they have both sides of the puzzle."

"I have talked to Anne about it, but she says they're going to wait five years. They can afford to do that because they're young. You can't."

"Thanks, Mother, it's always nice to be reminded that I'm getting older. By the way, we can't share a gynecologist anymore. Either you have to find a new one or I will."

"Why's that? I don't see any problem with it."

"The problem is that you have been discussing me with him. At my last checkup, he told me he had to keep a close eye on my reproductive health, or you would kill him. If anything should be off-limits, it's what I talk about with my GYN!" I got angry just thinking about it. Was nothing sacred?

"Well, there's no need to get upset, dear. I'm only concerned about you."

"No, you're concerned with whether I'm fertile or not. Mother, I've got to get ready. I'll see you in a little bit." I disconnected without further ado. She was completely exasperating. You'd think having a married brother would relieve some of the pressure about my having kids, but it didn't. If anything, she was worse.

Steve had not yet arrived at the church when I got there, so I had a few minutes to prepare myself before facing him after last night's make-out session. I plopped into my seat beside Anne and watched Mother making her rounds among the women across the aisle.

"So how'd the dinner go last night?" Anne asked.

I turned to face her. "Quite well, actually, except for the first and last bits."

She raised an eyebrow. "What would those be?"

"Brian showing up wanting to hang out because he was free, and then Steve kissing me good night at the door."

"Uh-oh."

I rolled my eyes. "Tell me about it." I told her the way I had treated Brian and went on to the kiss. "I thought if I could just kiss Steve, and kiss him I did, that I could put Brian out of my mind."

"Did it work?"

"Are you kidding?" I paused then said, "It gets worse. Brian knows I kissed him."

"How's that?"

I told her about rushing headlong over to Brian's house. "The worst part is that he said he didn't care who I kissed. Plus he's visiting that woman's church today." I made an ugly face to show just what I thought of that. "To top it all off, I slept horribly, again, and had a wonderful phone conversation with Mother bright and early this morning."

"Looks like you're in for another one," Anne warned. "She's headed this way now."

"You look lovely today, dear," Mother quipped cheerfully. This didn't bode well for me. She had something up her sleeve.

"Thank you," I said, giving her a peck.

"Since you said you weren't interested in dating Steve earlier, I've found another great guy for you to date. He's a friend of Louise's son. She gave him your number, so he'll be calling you sometime this week." Leave it to Mother to never give me a chance to say yes or no.

I was amazed, considering I'd thought she had run out of all available sons or friends of her contacts. "I'm not dating anyone, Mother. Please ask Louise to pass along the message to the friend." She stomped away in frustration, and Anne squeezed my hand in sympathy.

Much to my relief, Steve never did show up at church. The message light on my phone was blinking when I got home from dinner.

"Emma, it's Steve. I'm sorry I didn't make it to church, but I'm on my way to the airport. The office called, and I have to fly to Chicago. I'll be gone most of the week, but I'll call you when I get back. I love you." The answering machine clicked off.

I winced at his last words but breathed a sigh of relief. I was going to have to make it clear to him that we weren't dating each other, but at least it didn't have to be today. I decided to spend some time outdoors with Michelangelo and enjoy the somewhat cooler days we were having. We played fetch and chase until we were both exhausted, and then I curled up on the back porch with my legs beneath me to soak up some sunshine. My lack of restful sleep was catching up with me. I was getting drowsy, so I closed my eyes for just a minute and promptly fell asleep.

I don't know how long I had been asleep when it registered that someone's hand was on my face. I jerked awake and screamed like a banshee.

"Emma! It's Brian!" He gave me a little shake. I noticed that it was completely dark and much colder. I was shivering from fright, the cold, or probably both. "Let's get inside where it's warm." I started to stand, but my knees buckled. Luckily he had hold of my arm, or I'd have hit the ground.

"I think my legs are asleep," I stated.

He swooped me up in his arms as if I were light as a feather. "We'll take care of that." Things began to spin a little, so I put my arms around his neck and hid my face. *Please, God, don't let me faint. That would be too hard to explain.*

Brian carried me inside and deposited me on the couch, wrapping a quilt around my shoulders. He put some water on to boil and started taking off my shoes and socks.

"Wh-what are you doing?" I asked stupidly as he started rubbing his hands together briskly.

"Warming you up." He grinned.

He pushed one of my pant legs up over my knee and started massaging my calf. My heart skipped a beat as I tried to remember if I had shaved that morning. Whew! I had, but my heart rate remained elevated. He had great hands, firm but soft, with long fingers. They looked like the hands of a pianist, and right now he was playing a great tune on my skin. I couldn't tell if the tingles were from my legs coming back to life or his touch.

The kettle whistled shrilly, and he ran to the kitchen to take it off the stove. Then he came back to the couch and started on my other leg. "Hot tea on the way," he proclaimed proudly.

"Ow, ow, ow," I moaned.

He stopped. "Am I hurting you?"

"No, no. Keep going." I was definitely enjoying it. "I just hate the tingling. What makes it do that?"

"It's the blood rushing back to the areas you've deprived by sitting on your legs and cutting off the circulation." He grinned and kept massaging.

"You're a scream." I ruffled his hair. "Aren't you forget-ting something?"

"What?"

"The tea."

"Oh, yeah. Two sugars, right?"

He returned with my tea, pulled my legs up into his lap, and kept massaging, and I wasn't protesting even though my legs were fully awake.

"How's the tea?" he asked.

He'd brewed it too long, but I couldn't tell him that, espe-cially not since he'd remembered how I took it. "Perfect." I smiled, but he wasn't looking at me; he was looking at my feet. "What are you looking at?"

"You have really pretty feet."

"You think so?" I had painted my toenails again yester-day with my fire engine red polish. I was religious in using my pumice stone in the shower, so my soles were also cal-lous free.

"I do." He slid his hand down my leg and grasped my foot.

"Please don't," I gasped as my leg involuntarily jerked back.

"What's the matter?" he asked.

"It tickles."

"Really?" He grinned mischievously. "Is that the only place you're ticklish?"

I set my tea mug aside and pulled my legs off his lap to tuck them back under me. "Don't even think about it," I threatened.

"Or what?" He slid closer.

"Or I'll do something terrible."

He held his hands up like claws.

"Please, Brian," I begged, already beginning to giggle. "Please don't."

He pounced for my feet, grabbing them both and pinning them under his arm, tickling mercilessly. "This little piggy went to market."

He was laughing so hard he couldn't go on with the rhyme. I pounded on his back and kicked with all my might while shrieking my head off, but it was no use. Michelangelo was barking and bouncing around, wanting to get in on the game. Brian finally let go of my feet and turned with claws raised again.

"No, no more, please," I squealed. I tried to get up off the couch, but he grabbed me and started tickling my ribs relentlessly. I couldn't kick because my legs were pinned beneath him, but I was hitting him with one of the couch pillows and laughing hysterically. "Please, please stop! I'm going to pee my pants if you don't!"

He stopped tickling and rested his head on my stomach. I grabbed a fistful of his hair and gave him a little shake. Michelangelo finally settled back down.

I gave a deep, involuntary sigh of contentment. Looking up at me, Brian asked, "How are the legs now?"

I smiled and tousled his hair. "Quickly losing circulation since you're lying on top of them."

He freed my legs but kept his head on my stomach. He had great hair too, thick and wavy. I ran my fingers through it over and over as we lay there catching our breath. I gazed at the top of his head and wished with all my might that we could stay that way forever. This thought led to a delightful reverie, which I fully indulged for quite a while. Finally I gave myself a little shake back to the present as I leaned over a little to look at his face. Well, it would at least be for a little while longer, I thought. He had fallen asleep.

I reached for my copy of *Little Women* on the coffee table, careful not to wake him, and read in the silence, stroking my fingers through his hair and cherishing this moment with the man I loved.

I woke the next morning still on the couch and covered by a blanket. I had a vague memory of Brian covering me and kissing my cheek before leaving. Trying to stretch the kinks out of my back, I thought back over the previous evening. It had almost been like old times between us except for the little inconvenience of my being in love with him.

I didn't want to get up, but Michelangelo needed out. He headed for the nearest tree, and I took my tea mug to the dishwasher, pouring what was left in the pot down the sink. It really had been terrible tea, but he was a sweetheart to have tried.

I made it to the bookstore before Kathy for once, even after stopping at Starbucks. I was beginning to get worried when she floated through the door shortly before nine. I handed her a latté and raised an eyebrow. "Rough weekend?"

"Honey, I think I'm in love," she said dramatically with one hand on her heart.

"Donnie?"

"Yes, ma'am. We had the best time together on Friday, so we spent Saturday and Sunday together too."

I raised my eyebrow even higher. "All weekend?"

"Well, he went home at night," she said, quickly catching on to my meaning. "What kind of girl do you take me for?"

I laughed as she blushed. "I'm just kidding, Kathy. That's really great."

"What about your weekend?"

I told her about Steve and the opera. "I think he's growing up."

"Well, I'll say this much for him; he certainly knows how to show a girl a good time. How are things with Brian?"

"Okay, I guess. Things were almost normal last night."

"That's good, isn't it?"

"As good as it can be under the circumstances. Are you and Donnie going out again this weekend?" I needed to change the subject.

"Actually I'm meeting him for dinner tonight."

"Wow, four days in a row. Don't you want to play the field a little more?"

"Well, I'm not getting any younger, and I don't want to spend all my time flitting from man to man."

"You're not that much older than me," I protested.

"Honey, you're too kind. I'm a good ten years older than you."

"Well, I'm happy for you." I couldn't help the little pang of envy I felt at the way she happily hummed love songs through the rest of the day.

Chapter Nine

THE NEXT FEW days passed quickly. Kathy and Donnie continued to see each other every day, and she regaled me with all of their doings. Brian and I had fallen back into our normal routine except that I had to hear a lot of talk about Delilah. I was just glad to be able to keep my feelings hidden from him.

Steve had called me twice from Chicago to chat, and John and I had exchanged several e-mails. He was still asking to see the books, but I wasn't completely comfortable with that idea although I wasn't sure why. It was a reasonable request from a collector.

The phone rang on Thursday evening as I was sitting down to watch my favorite television drama. *Thank goodness for TiVo*, I thought as I answered, "Hello?"

"Hi, is this Emma Bailey?"

"Yes, it is," I answered, mystified by the unfamiliar male voice.

"This is Brad Clayton. I'm supposed to be your blind date this weekend."

Mother obviously had not relayed the message. "Oh, hello, Brad. How are you?"

"I'm great. You?"

"I'm fine. I'm terribly sorry, but there seems to have been some miscommunication."

"What do you mean?"

For a moment I considered making up some imaginary plans, then I decided it wasn't worth the trouble. Better to just tell the truth. "My mother is aware that I recently made the decision to no longer date anyone. I asked her to inform Louise of that decision, but obviously the message has gone astray."

"You're kidding, right?" He chuckled.

"No, I'm not. I am not interested in dating anyone."

"I get it." He didn't sound happy. "You're one of those women's lib man-haters, eh?"

"Good night, Brad." I hung up the phone.

I was able to watch the first ten minutes of my show before the phone rang again. I pressed the pause button, a little exasperated. "Hello?"

"How's my girl?"

That little question was getting irritating. "Hello, Steve. How are things in Chicago?"

"Almost wrapped up, which is why I'm calling. I'll be back in town a week from Saturday, so what do you want to do that evening?"

Uh-oh. It was time for "the conversation." "Listen, Steve. I think you've got the wrong idea about us."

"We're back together. How's that the wrong idea?"

I rolled my eyes. "Because we're not back together, we're just friends. I never said that I wanted to date you. In fact, you should be dating because I'm not going to make that kind of commitment to anyone again."

"To me, you mean." His voice was flat.

"No, I'd say the same thing to anyone." That was the truth, but only because I wasn't dating Brian.

"Fine. I'll wait until you are ready to commit because I don't want anybody else but you."

"That's not going to happen, Steve. I'm sorry," I said and hung up the phone. I thought that was the best way to end that conversation. I hit the play button and finally finished watching my show.

Kathy and I worked later than usual on Friday to catch up on inventory after the big sale. We actually spent more time talking about our weekend plans than getting any work done. She and Donnie were still going strong. I was happy for her, but a little tiny part of me couldn't help but be envious.

I grabbed some Chinese takeout on the way home and spent a quiet evening in bed with Michelangelo watching the classics yet again. Brian was out with Delilah, and I was spending another night with his sweatshirt. I hadn't returned it yet, and it still held his scent. After I finished the takeout and half a pint of ice cream, I decided to get to bed early. No need to look like a zombie at church tomorrow.

꙳

I spent another night tossing and turning with all manner of torturous thoughts spinning through my head. I took Michelangelo to the backyard before showering the next morning. I dressed carefully, just in case Delilah would be there again; I couldn't suffer by comparison. I was arranging my hair when the doorbell rang. Brian was standing there with a bag in his hand.

"What's in the bag?" I asked curiously.

"Chocolate éclairs."

"Bless you!" I grabbed his arm and pulled him inside before grabbing the bag out of his hand and heading for the kitchen. "Milk?" I asked.

"Definitely." We sat at the table, and I poured him a glass of milk while he dug the éclairs out of the bag.

"Mmm," I sighed as I took the first bite and the Bavarian cream filling oozed out of the pastry. "Thank you for this."

"You're welcome." He handed me a napkin.

I took a few more bites for fortitude and then plunged in. "I figured you'd be on your way to see Delilah this morning, or is she coming to church?" *Please say no.*

"Actually she's out of town this week, so I'm flying solo."

Yes! "Oh, is she on vacation?" I feigned both interest and calm.

"No, she's at a conference in Chicago."

"What are you going to do with yourself all week?"

"Well, I thought I'd hang out with my best friend and get caught up on her life." He grinned.

"That sounds like a great plan, but who's this best friend you're talking about?" I asked innocently.

He balled up his napkin and threw it at me. "The crazy redhead who lives next door to me."

I threw the napkin back at him. "Thanks a lot."

"So you want to ride to church with me?"

"Sure. Just let me go repair the damage your éclairs have done to my lipstick."

We joked and laughed all the way to church. He threw his arm around my shoulders as we walked toward the building. "I'm glad to see you back to your normal self today."

"What do you mean?" I asked indignantly.

"Well, you've been awfully quiet the last few weeks." His eyes were full of concern.

"Have I?" Crap, I was going to have to do a better acting job around him. "I didn't mean to be. Just a lot on my mind, I guess."

"Then I guess I'm going to have to do a better job of taking your mind off things, as your best friend." He gave me a friendly embrace.

"I'll take you up on that offer." I laughed and hugged him back. We were still laughing as we walked into the sanctuary with his arm around me.

Anne arrived and sat on the other side of Brian. Teddy was passing out bulletins. She leaned forward so she could see me and asked, "How was your weekend?"

I moved closer to Brian so that we could keep our voices down, or so I told myself. "Horrific."

Anne's eyes widened. "What happened?"

I told them both about Mother's failed blind date attempt, and we were all laughing by the time I was through. I also told them about my conversation with Steve.

"Way to go, Emma," Brian said as he gave my leg a pat.

Mother was sitting on the other side of Teddy, having made her rounds among the ladies of the church, but she was ignoring me as punishment for not going on the blind date. All I could think was that I could use this kind of punishment more often.

❦

Dinner would have been unbearable had it not been for Brian. He'd always had a way with my mother, and he never failed to smooth her feathers when they got ruffled, which I had certainly done. I listened in awe as he talked to her about my strength and actually portrayed me as a hero of womanhood for my actions.

We finished eating and helped Mother clear the table. Brian and I took our leave of the family and walked back to his car. Once seated inside, I started applauding. "Bravo! You had her eating out of your hand. I don't know how you do it."

He made a seated bow. "Ah, it was nothing. You just have to put it in words she can understand."

I laughed. "Yeah, words like *valiant, noble, passionate,* etc."

"Hey, whatever works, right?"

I leaned back into my seat. "So what do you want to do since you're footloose and fancy free?"

"Let's go to the park."

"Great idea."

He pulled a blanket from the trunk of his car, and we set off to find a good place to spread it out. We pulled off our shoes and plopped down.

"So what's really going on with you and Steve?" He was lying on his back watching the clouds as the breeze played with the waves in his hair.

"What do you mean?" I was on my stomach, chin in my hands, just drinking in the sight of him.

"Are you getting serious about him again?" He looked over at me, waiting for my answer.

I tried to ignore the churning in my stomach caused by his gaze. "No. I thought we could be friends, but I don't think that's going to work on his side." Quickly I changed the subject. "What about Delilah? Are you guys serious?" *Please say no*, I begged silently.

He looked up at the sky thoughtfully. "I think we could be." My heart almost failed me. Then he continued. "It's a little early to know for sure." Nothing was definite, thank goodness. "But I'm also not dating anyone else." My stomach plummeted.

"So tell me more about her," I said, in conflict. I didn't want to hear anything about her, but I had to know what he saw in her.

He rolled on his side to look at me. "She's so sweet and caring. She's very close to her family, and she shares your love of books." I gave him a little smile. "Most people would think we wouldn't get along because she's so creative, like you, and I'm so logical. I guess it's true that opposites attract."

"I guess." I shrugged and looked away. "I'm certainly no expert."

"None of us are," he said quietly. When I didn't respond, he asked in a more lighthearted tone, "So does your mother have another blind date planned for this weekend?"

"Not that I know of." I told him about John being in town next weekend. "We'll probably have dinner one evening, but that's about it." We were silent for a while as the sky grew dark and the temperature dropped a little.

"Are you getting cold?" he asked finally.

I was pretty content. "Not too bad."

"Well, if you can hold out a little while longer, roll up in your side of the blanket and scoot over here. I want you to see something before we leave."

"What?" I asked as I rolled closer.

"It's a surprise." We waited a few minutes and then he pointed at the sky. "Look! There!" It was a shooting star. "Quick! Make a wish."

I closed my eyes and wished with all my might that Brian would learn to love me instead of Delilah. I opened my eyes again and tried to see his eyes in the moonlight. "You couldn't possibly have known that there would be a shooting star tonight."

I could barely make out his grin in the twilight. "Oh, but I could. Don't you know I have secret powers?"

"Yeah, right. Now what gives?"

He was laughing. "They said on the news last night that there would be a meteor shower tonight. Look!" He pointed at the sky again, and I stared in wonder as a shower of sparkling stars streaked across the sky.

We finally left the park and headed to my house for some hot chocolate. "Want to watch a movie?" I asked as I placed our mugs in the sink. I didn't want the evening to end.

"Rain check? I told Delilah I'd call her tonight, and it's getting late."

Drat that woman! "Sure," I replied with nonchalance. "You know where to find me."

"Thanks for the hot chocolate." He gave me a swift peck on the cheek. "See ya, babe."

"Thanks for the stars, Brian." He was laughing on his way out the door.

I gave Michelangelo his supper and put on another Keith Urban CD before settling in bed with *Little Women*. The music suited my mood, and I knew the book would distract my mind for a little while anyway. The ringing of the phone woke me. I glanced at the clock and groaned. I'd only been asleep a few minutes, and I needed some rest after all these restless nights.

"Hello?"

"Emma, this is John."

I gave my head a shake to clear it. "John, it's good to hear from you. How are you?"

"Great. I just wanted to let you know that I'll fly into Dallas late on Friday. Would you be free for dinner on Saturday evening?"

"That would be wonderful."

"Good. What's your favorite food?"

Didn't have to think about that one. "Definitely Italian."

"What do you know, it's mine, too, and I know a great little place. Shall I pick you up?"

Even though this wouldn't qualify for the blind date escape transportation theory, I didn't know him very well either. "Why don't I meet you there?"

"Okay." He sounded disappointed. "It's called Mario's. Have you heard of it?"

"I've never eaten there, but I know where it is. What time should we meet?"

"Is six o'clock all right?"

"Perfect."

"Then it's a date. I can't wait to see you again."

"Me too. Good night." I hung up the phone and replayed my evening with Brian. It had almost been perfect. Almost.

Chapter Ten

KATHY AND I were getting ready to close up on Friday evening when Donnie came walking through the door. Kathy hurried from behind the counter to give him a hug. I took a good look at him as they approached the counter with arms around each other. He was of average height, which was a good thing since Kathy was on the shorter side. He had black hair and blue eyes and wore glasses with black plastic frames. Most people would have described his looks as nerdy—but then he took off his glasses. The transformation from nerd to hunk was astounding.

"Emma, this is Donnie Richards. Donnie, this is Emma." Kathy was beaming.

"Donnie, I've heard a lot about you," I said as I shook his hand. "It's a pleasure to finally meet you."

He gave me a warm smile that I couldn't help but return. "You too. Kathy talks about you all the time."

"I consider myself very lucky to have a friend like her."

"Me too," he said, hugging her closer. "Have you told her?" he asked Kathy.

"Told me what?" My heart skipped a beat. For a moment I thought she was going to tell me they were engaged.

Kathy grinned as if she'd read my mind. "Donnie and I are having a costume party next Saturday for Halloween.

We'd love for you to join us, and of course you can invite someone as your date."

I was thrilled. "I'd love to come. You know I can't resist any reason for dressing up." The bell over the door rang again, and I looked up to see my neighbor/best friend standing in the doorway. "Brian!" I exclaimed in surprise.

Kathy turned around. "Brian, how are you? Long time no see."

He strolled over to us. "Yeah, I've been busy, but it's great to see you again. Is this Donnie?"

Kathy made introductions and spoke again. "Donnie and I are having a costume party next weekend for Halloween. We'd like for you to be there."

"Can I bring someone with me?"

"Of course." Kathy gave me a smile.

"I'm sure Delilah would love it."

Kathy looked back at Brian in surprise but quickly composed her features. I think she had forgotten about Delilah. "Great," she said, trying to sound enthusiastic.

"Who are you going to bring, Emma?" Donnie asked politely.

"Oh, just me, I guess."

"Kathy, honey, we should get going if you're ready." Donnie gave her hand a squeeze. "We have reservations for six."

"Let me just grab my things." She came around the counter to where I was standing while Donnie and Brian stood talking a few feet away. "I'm so sorry, Emma," she whispered. "I should have just kept my big mouth shut and let you ask Brian about the party so you could have come together."

I shrugged. "Don't worry about it. I'm sure it'll be fun. By the way, Donnie's a dreamboat."

"Isn't he? Oh, Emma. I know we've only been seeing each other for a few weeks, but I really think I love that man."

"I'm happy for you, Kathy. Truly I am." I gave her a hug. "Now go. I can see he's anxious to have you all to himself." In fact, Donnie couldn't keep his eyes off of her.

Donnie and Kathy said good-bye and left. I stayed behind the counter to finish totaling the receipts but watched Brian as he browsed through the shelves. "So what brings you here tonight?" I finally asked, putting the receipts away.

"Well, I'm going to see my parents this evening, and I thought I'd see if you wanted to come along. It's been a while since you've seen them, and they've been asking about you."

Brian's parents were two of my favorite people. From the first time I had met them, they had insisted that I call them Mom and Dad. "Everyone else does, dear," his mother had told me. They had accepted me into their family with open arms even though I was just his friend.

"I would love it. I've missed them too."

I locked up the store, and he followed me home so I could get Michelangelo settled outside with his supper and drop off my car. Brian's parents lived about two hours away on their horse ranch. Brian's father was an excellent businessman and had been able to retire with a nice fortune due to his successful ventures. Horses were his hobby, so he'd bought the ranch and built a lovely home. It reminded me of Tara from *Gone with the Wind*, and I loved it.

As we walked up the drive, Mr. Davis opened the door and called over his shoulder, "Momma, your baby's home, and he's got someone with him." As I stepped into the pool of light from the old-fashioned lantern by the front door, he shouted back, "It's Emma!" He grabbed me in a bear hug that almost took my breath away before holding me at arm's length. "Let's get a good look at you. Where have you been, girl? I do believe you're getting thinner. We need to fatten you up, or you're gonna blow away." He looked just like an older version of his son.

Mrs. Davis was busy hugging her youngest son, but she replied, "I'll take care of that in no time." She pushed her husband out of the way and took me in her arms. "Emma, it's so good to see you. Brian, you should bring her around more often. I miss this dear girl when I don't get to see her." She was a petite woman with soft brown hair and twinkly eyes. She'd always reminded me of John Arbuckle's mother in the *Garfield* comic strip.

"I've missed you too." I gave her another hug.

"Well, let's not stand here all night. Dinner's almost ready; I just have to mash the potatoes. Emma, you come on with me to the kitchen. You men just go watch your football or whatever it is, so we can talk."

I followed her down the hall and sat on a stool at the bar. "What can I do to help, Mom?"

"Not a thing, other than to start talking. I assume you've met Delilah?"

I nodded.

"Well, I don't like her," she said, mashing potatoes with a vengeance.

I was startled for a second by the thought that Brian had introduced Delilah to his parents without telling me. "You've met her then?" I asked in dismay.

"Not yet," she answered, "but I don't like what she's done to my boy."

I was relieved that Brian hadn't brought her to meet them yet. That meant he still wasn't serious enough about her. "What do you mean, what she's done to Brian?"

"Since he's started dating that woman, he's become moody. He mopes when he's here, and he's too quiet. She can't be good for him."

That was funny. I hadn't noticed his being moody. "I know he's been busy at work. Maybe he's preoccupied with that."

"No. It didn't begin until he started dating that woman." The potatoes got two more slams with the masher.

"Well, he's seemed happy every time I've seen him," I said hesitantly.

"I'm sure he is when he's with you. You've always been good for him. He was telling me just the other day how much you've changed, standing up for yourself and being so strong. He said it was like he was meeting a whole new you." She put down the pot and looked at me wistfully. "I know you two have always said you were just friends, but I always hoped that…" Her voice trailed away.

She'd never told me that before. I was touched, especially considering how my feelings had changed toward her son. Tears sprang to my eyes as I buried my face in my hands.

She hurried around the island to fold me into her arms. "Emma, dear, what is it?"

"Oh, Mom, I'm in love with him."

She patted my back and spoke soothing words while we both cried together. "Have you told him?" she finally asked.

"I can't. He doesn't feel the same way, and I can't ruin our friendship."

"Maybe he just needs a wake-up call to make him realize that he feels the same way."

"I don't think so, Mom, and I can't take that chance. He seems pretty wrapped up in Delilah to me."

"That woman!" was all she said. She patted her tears away with her apron. "You better go repair your appearance, dear, before Brian sees and starts asking questions."

"Please don't say anything to him about this," I begged.

"Don't you worry, honey. Much as I'd like to, I won't say a word, but I'm sure gonna do a lot of praying."

I freshened myself up in the bathroom and joined everyone in the dining room. The meal was delicious, and Mr. Davis kept us laughing with stories about his ranch hands and the horses. I helped Mom clear the table, and then we joined Brian and his father in the living room with cups of coffee and caught up on what had been happening in our lives.

Before we knew it, we were all yawning, and it was quite late. Brian stood up. "I guess we should be going," he said.

"Don't try to make the drive tonight," Mom begged. "I'll worry about you all night. Just stay, and y'all can leave after I make breakfast. There's plenty of room here."

Brian looked at me questioningly. Mom was right. Brian had four older siblings, all of whom were married and out of the house, so their rooms were free. "It's all right with me," I said. "Michelangelo will be okay outside, and I don't have plans until tomorrow night."

"Okay, Mom. We'll stay."

"Good. Emma, you can stay in Mary's room, and Brian, you know your way around the house. What would everyone like for breakfast?"

Brian and his dad looked at each other before answering in unison, "Biscuits and cocoa gravy."

Mom took me to Brian's older sister's bedroom where I would stay the night and pulled a long nightgown from one of the dresser drawers. Mary's many piano trophies lined a shelf on one wall, and mementos from her school years were hung everywhere. A huge canopy bed filled the center of the room with bedding the color of sunshine. It looked young and girlish.

"There are towels and washcloths in the linen closet in the bathroom. Just make yourself at home and help yourself to anything you need, dear." She came closer and gave me a hug. "Don't worry about you and Brian. Things will come right in the end; I just know it."

"Thanks, Mom. Good night."

"'Night, dear." She left the room, closing the door softly behind her.

I spent a few minutes looking at the pictures of Mary's friends and family on the walls before getting ready for bed. Brian was in several, although he'd been much younger. Even then, he'd been a good-looking kid. I smiled as I looked at him and thought of the man he had become; he'd only gotten better with age.

I had just changed into the nightgown and slipped into bed when I heard a soft tap on the door. Brian stuck his head inside and whispered, "Are you decent?"

"Yes," I whispered back, and he came inside holding a tray with two glasses of milk and peanut butter cookies.

"Contraband," he said, laughing softly as he shut the door behind him and brought the tray over to the bed. I took the glasses of milk and held them while he climbed onto the other side of bed. He passed me a cookie, and I handed him a glass.

"Your mother will have a heart attack if she catches you in here."

He waggled his eyebrows and bit into a cookie. "I'll be sure to leave just before dawn." He laughed at my horrified expression, and I threatened to hit him with a pillow. "So what were you and Mom talking about in the kitchen all that time?"

That's why he'd brought the milk and cookies; he was on a hunt for information. "Oh, just girl talk."

"That means you were talking about someone." He rolled his eyes. "Anyone in particular?"

I took a drink of milk to give myself time to consider how to answer. I decided to tell a little of the truth. "We were talking about you, actually."

He looked surprised. "Really? What about me?"

"Well, she's concerned about you."

"Why?" He was frowning a little and playing with his glass.

"She says you've been very quiet lately."

He looked up at me. "Have I?" He set his glass on the nightstand.

"I hadn't noticed it, but she would certainly know you better than I do. Mothers and their youngest sons always share a special bond, I've been told."

He looked away. "I guess I've just had a lot on my mind lately."

I set my glass aside and snuggled under the covers on my side so that I could see still see him. "Like what?" I asked.

"Delilah, for one. She wants me to spend Thanksgiving with her family."

My stomach lurched. "But what about your mom and dad? They'd be so upset if you weren't here."

"I know, but I'm not ready to bring her over here to meet them yet, and I'm afraid that if I say no, she'll be upset." He plopped back against the pillows.

I was glad to hear he was still taking things slowly. It would be a huge step for Brian to bring the girl he was dating home to meet his parents. A suggestion formed in my mind, and the words came out almost against my will. "Maybe you could do both: have dinner with your family first and then meet her at her family's."

He still wouldn't look at me. "Maybe, but I'm not sure she'll be satisfied with that."

"Well, don't they always say that couples have to learn to compromise?"

"Normally that's true, but Delilah doesn't always see it that way."

It sounded to me like Miss Delilah was a pain in the butt, but I couldn't very well tell him that, so I just kept silent for a minute. "You said Delilah was one thing that was on your mind. What's the other?"

He rolled over on his side to face me and said simply, "You."

I wasn't prepared for that. I stammered, "M-me? What for?"

"I know you've been having a hard time lately with your family and Steve after your decision, and I haven't been around as much as usual since I've started dating Delilah."

Now I couldn't meet his eyes as I said, "I'm okay, Brian. Really."

He tilted my chin with his hand so that I had to look at him. "Are you? I mean, you're definitely stronger than you were, but is your life the way you want it? Sometimes it seems to me like you've jumped headlong into spinsterhood just to get away from something I can't quite put my finger on. Other times, I get the feeling that you don't like Delilah."

The man was too perceptive for his own good. I closed my eyes for a moment, summoning all the courage and strength I had to look him in the eye. I decided to ignore the questions about me and only address the Delilah issue. I took his hand where it lay between us and said, "I've had you to myself for so long that I just have to adjust to sharing you with someone else. It would be that way no matter who it was, Brian. If she truly makes you happy, then I'm happy for you." I gave him a smile, and he squeezed my hand in return.

"Good night, Emma." He gave me a peck on the cheek before sliding off the bed. "Don't let the bedbugs bite."

"You too, Brian." Then he was out the door, and I was doomed to another sleepless night.

The next morning we shared a huge breakfast with Brian's parents before they walked us to the car. Mr. Davis gave me another bear hug. "Don't stay away so long, young lady. You're welcome anytime."

"Thanks, Dad."

Mom took me in her arms and whispered, "Hang in there." Then she stepped away while I got in the car. "Emma, dear, you have to come back on Thanksgiving. I'm making a pumpkin cheesecake just for you."

"I'll be on my way as soon as we finish dinner at the parsonage."

I blew one last kiss to Mr. Davis as Brian pulled out of the drive. We were both silent most of the way home. "So you're having dinner with John this evening?" he asked as he pulled into the driveway in front of his house.

"Yeah. Is Delilah back from her conference?"

"She was supposed to have gotten in early this morning. I'm going over to her place for supper."

We got out of the car, and I gave him a one-armed hug. "Well, have fun, and thanks for asking me along last night."

"You're welcome. I hope your dinner goes well."

Michelangelo was extremely happy to see me. I gave him an extra helping of food to keep him occupied while I went to brush my teeth and take a shower and then give myself a manicure and pedicure while letting my hair dry and watching part of the Alfred Hitchcock marathon on TV.

By the time everything finished drying, it was almost time to meet John at the restaurant. I slipped into a red wrap dress and put the finishing touches on my hair before grabbing my purse and heading out the door.

John was waiting for me as I entered the restaurant. "Emma, it's so nice to see you again. You look beautiful." He kissed my cheek and spoke to the hostess, who escorted us to a secluded booth. He was quite dashing in a blue pin-striped suit and silk tie.

"So how are things in New York?" I asked after we had gotten menus.

"Business is booming, although my client is still interested in those books of yours."

"Sorry, but they're still not for sale." I smiled and looked back at the menu. "Everything sounds delicious. I'm terrible at making decisions."

"Allow me to choose for you?" he asked.

"Be my guest."

The waitress came back to our table, and John ordered bruschetta for our appetizer, salad, and chicken roma for the main course. Everything was delicious. John was an excellent conversationalist and told me all about the different places to which he had traveled for his clients.

"You weren't lying when you said you had to do a lot of traveling," I commented.

"Some of it is very enjoyable, but it can also get tiresome. My intention is to work as much as I can now so that I can retire early and travel solely for pleasure."

"That's a great plan. I think we'd all like to do the same."

Smiling, he reached across the table to take my hand. "Maybe it'll work out so that we can do some of that traveling together."

I smiled uncomfortably. After all, we hadn't known each other very long and already he was talking about traveling together. I withdrew my hand as the waitress appeared with our dessert and cappuccino. After she left, we continued to talk about the places that we would like to visit the most. He wanted to take as much time as necessary to see every item in the Louvre in Paris, and I wanted to visit all the castles in Europe.

We were halfway through our dessert of tiramisu when he reached for his side and pulled a pager off his belt. He checked the number. "I'm terribly sorry, Emma, but I must take this call."

"Of course." I watched as he walked to the bar and spoke briefly on the phone.

He returned to the table with a frown on his handsome face. "I'm sorry, Emma, but my mother has fallen ill. I must return to New York immediately."

"Oh, John, I'm so sorry. Of course, I understand."

He leaned forward and said earnestly, "I really wanted to spend some more time with you. I should be back in Dallas again in a few weeks. May I see you then?"

"Sure," I replied. After all, we never had discussed business.

He took care of the check and escorted me to my car. "I'm so sorry to have to cut our evening short."

"John, please don't worry about it. I just hope your mother gets better."

"My moth—oh, yes. I'll call you soon." He leaned down and kissed my cheek. "Good night, Emma."

I got into my car and drove away. This evening certainly had ended unexpectedly. Then again, that seemed to be the only constant in my life these days: the unexpected.

Everything was dark at Brian's house when I pulled into my driveway. He must have already gone to Delilah's. I changed into my pajamas and spent another evening with Michelangelo in my bed and Cary Grant on the television.

I tossed and turned all night and finally crawled out of bed at seven the next morning. I passed on coffee, although I didn't really believe it was caffeine causing my problem.

I had a glass of orange juice with a bagel instead and spent a leisurely hour reading the newspaper until I reached the page where engagements and weddings were announced. I couldn't help but read about the couples and the brides, who were all in their early twenties. I crumpled the pictures of their smiling faces in my hands, rapidly feeling old.

Gathering the rest of the newspaper in my arms, I dumped it into the trashcan on the way to let Michelangelo out. Then I took a long shower, soaking up the warmth and trying to scrub away my anxiety. While my skin was still moist, I rubbed my favorite lotion over every inch of my body, which I didn't always take the time to do. It smelled like magnolias and clean linen.

I was feeling better until I looked in the mirror. Two sleepless nights in a row had taken their toll on my face. Truth was I hadn't been sleeping well since I had realized I was in love with Brian. My eyes were bloodshot and hollow with bluish shadows beneath them, and my faced looked drained of color. Worst of all, I also noticed the beginnings of fine lines around my eyes.

I splashed my face with cold water several times to bring some semblance of life back to my cheeks. Better, but I'd definitely have to apply my makeup carefully. I squeezed a couple of drops of Visine in each eye and headed toward my closet to dress, choosing a vibrant red pantsuit that would hopefully draw people's eyes away from my haggard appearance.

After finally deciding that I looked good enough to go out in public, I gathered my things and went to church. I was early, and the sanctuary was empty except for the pianist, who was practicing for that morning's service. I sat in our pew and closed my eyes, listening to the beautiful music. Then I bowed my head and prayed silently. *Help me to be patient. Help me to accept what happens in my life. Give me peace. Let me sleep tonight.*

I felt someone sit down beside me. "Emma, are you okay?"

Steve's beautiful blue eyes were so full of concern.

"I'm fine," I said. "Just spending some quiet time with my conscience."

He settled his arm around me. "How was your weekend?"

"Pretty good. Yours?"

His answer surprised me. "A quiet party at home for one."

"That reminds me. Kathy and her new boyfriend are having a costume party next weekend. Would you like to go?"

"I'm afraid I can't. I made plans with some friends."

The music was so soothing. I closed my eyes again just to rest them.

From some distance away, I heard someone ask, "Is she okay?" Funny, it sounded like Delilah.

"I think she's asleep." Why would Steve be talking to Delilah?

"Emma?" That was definitely Brian, and he was shaking my shoulder gently.

I opened one eye and groaned. The entire family was standing around me and staring. God had answered my prayer about sleep a little too early. I sat up and saw Delilah laughing behind her hand. Crap!

"Emma, are you okay?" Brian asked again.

"I'm fine." I turned back to Steve. "I'm sorry. I just haven't been sleeping well lately."

"You can use my shoulder for your pillow anytime." He was laughing at me; they all were except Anne and Brian.

"It's not funny," Brian hissed. The vein in his temple was throbbing. He took my arm and helped me stand. "We should get you home. You need to be in bed."

"But, Brian, what about church?" Delilah whined.

"I'm fine, y'all," I said, embarrassed. "Forget about it."

Mother leaned forward, as if examining me. "You obviously need some rest. You look dreadful."

"Thanks, Mother."

"I can take you home, Emma," Steve said.

I looked at Anne with pleading in my eyes. "No, Steve," she said, taking charge of the situation. "I'll take Emma home. You stay for church." She walked over and took my arm. "Teddy, I'll meet you back at the parsonage for lunch."

He kissed her cheek. "Take care, Emma."

I gave him a half-smile as Anne turned to Brian. "Brian, can you bring her car home afterwards?" she asked.

"Absolutely."

Delilah was pouting as I handed over my keys, but Brian didn't seem to notice as he removed the car key from the ring. "I'll check on you later, Emma," he said, giving my hand a squeeze.

Anne maneuvered me out of the pew, and I felt my face redden as I realized that everyone in the church had been watching this little scene play out. Whispers and laughter followed us out the door; I could only imagine what people were thinking, although I knew it would be the worst.

Anne drove me home and got me settled into bed with a cup of tea. "Okay, why aren't you sleeping?"

I giggled a little. "I am. Just not at the appropriate time."

"You know what I mean. What's on your mind, Emma?"

Suddenly nothing seemed funny. "Everything," I blurted. I told her about the conversations I'd had with Brian on the night of the shooting stars and the evening at his parents' house. "I'm worried about Brian because I'm afraid he's getting serious about Delilah and that she's going to end up hurting him. I'm worried about me if they do get serious because I don't know that I'll be able to forget my feelings for Brian." My words had gotten faster and faster as my anxiety rose.

"Take a breather, and drink your tea before it gets cold," Anne advised.

I took a few obedient sips. "I'm not the only one that's worried either. Brian's mother is worried about him too." I repeated her concerns.

When I finished, Anne was shaking her head. "Emma, do you realize you're worrying about all these things that you can't possibly control? You can't change other people's feelings."

"Logically I know that, but emotionally I've run amuck."

Her tone softened. "Personally I think you've been doing a pretty great job. You've been supportive of Brian without interfering. You've accepted your feelings for him and managed to keep your friendship intact. Plus you're becoming a strong, self-sufficient person."

I grimaced. "You make me sound like a saint."

"No, just a pretty fantastic woman." She patted my knee. "Now you need to get some sleep."

"Thanks, Anne. It helps just to talk about it with you. You're so rational." I yawned and snuggled down under the covers smiling. She'd already made me feel better.

"Now you make *me* sound like a saint." She took the empty teacup from my hands.

I burrowed under the covers, hearing the clicking of Michelangelo's nails on the kitchen tile. Anne must have let him in before leaving. He placed his nose on the edge of the bed and sniffed my face a few times. I patted the bed, and he jumped up beside me. With my hand on his side, I fell asleep to the steady rhythm of his breathing.

❦

Someone's hand was smoothing the hair out of my face. It was so gentle and comforting. The fingertips were soft as butterfly wings.

"Brian?" I opened my eyes briefly to see his face close to mine.

"Shh. Go back to sleep," he whispered, and I felt the softness of his lips on mine. I slept through the night.

Chapter Eleven

I AWOKE THE next morning wondering if I had dreamed it all, but there were my car keys on my nightstand. Brian must have been there checking up on me like he'd said he would, but that part about the kiss had to have been wishful dreaming on my part. Too bad.

Before heading to work, I took a few minutes to go through the pile of mail I had been neglecting the last few days. On the bottom, I found the envelope containing my concealed handgun license. The picture was almost as bad as the one on my driver's license, but at least it was here.

I put the license in my wallet and went back to my bedroom to get the gun case out of the drawer of my nightstand. I checked the gun to make sure that everything was in order, that the clip was full, and that the safety was on. After assuring myself that everything was secure, I placed it in my purse and made sure the outline wasn't visible. I was ready to carry.

Driving to the bookstore, I walked through the door and pointed my fingers like a gun at Kathy behind the counter. Doing the best Dirty Harry imitation I could, which wasn't saying much, I said, "You've got to ask yourself one question—'Do I feel lucky?' Well? Do ya, punk?"

She started laughing. "Oh no. Dirty Harriet's on the warpath, which means you must have gotten your license. Congratulations."

"Correct. Fear not, fair maiden. I can protect you—as long as we're together anyway." I put my purse under the counter and laughed at Kathy's expression. She was looking at it as if it were filled with something completely disgusting. "It's not going to hurt you just sitting there, Kathy."

"Well, just keep it out of sight. We don't want to scare off the customers or anything."

"I don't know. It might be fun to scare off Mrs. Bagley." Mrs. Bagley was an annoying customer who complained about every book she bought for her daughter.

For a moment Kathy looked as if she might be considering it as well. "Nah, better just leave it hidden. The sight of it would probably kill her instead of just giving her a scare."

I rolled my eyes. "With my luck, you're probably right."

Still watching my purse out of the corner of her eye, Kathy asked, "So how'd your weekend go?"

"I fell asleep at church, if that's any indication."

"Not good."

"To say the least." I filled her in on all the messy details. "So what can I do to help with the party? I've got plenty of time on my hands this week."

"Would you take care of the food? You make such great hors d'oeuvres."

"Sure."

"Great. Just make me a grocery list, and I'll have it all waiting at the house. I'll take care of the decorations, and Donnie said he'd get the music together. He's a deejay on the side."

"Wow." I was impressed. "This should be a great party then. What are you going to be?"

"We're going to be Gomez and Morticia Addams."

"Hey! You could borrow that black wig I have."

Her eyes lit up. "You're right! Thanks. What about you?"

"I'm going to be a flapper from the Roaring Twenties. I've already got the costume."

"I can't wait to see it. Has Brian said what he and Delilah are going to be?"

"No, but I'm sure Miss Delilah will look perfect."

Kathy folded her arms and said without expression, "You know, I can't imagine her at a costume party."

I knew exactly what she meant. "Neither can I."

We spent the next several days splitting our time between the bookstore and Kathy's house. By Friday, all the decorations were up, and the house looked great. There were candles everywhere because Kathy wanted to keep the lights dimmed. "Bright lights destroy the mood I'm trying to create," she quipped. Spider webs and big, hairy fake spiders were hiding in unexpected places, which completely freaked me out. Spiders of any kind made me hysterical, and Donnie had many laughs at my expense.

I had made as many nibbles as Kathy's refrigerator could hold: a cheese ball and crackers, a vegetable tray with a ranch dip, stuffed mushrooms, a variety of sandwiches, different kinds of shrimp, and lots of homemade cookies. Mr. Chen's Chinese Takeout would be getting a lot of business from me because I wouldn't be interested in cooking again for a while.

Once the food was ready, I left Kathy's to go home and get ready for the party. I took my costume out of the bag and gave it a shake. It was a fabulous red satin dress with rows and rows of fringe and spaghetti straps. Long red satin gloves, black heels, a knotted string of fake pearls, and a black cigarette holder with a fake cigarette completed the outfit.

I went into the bathroom and pulled my curls into a small bun in order to tuck them under the wig, which was shaped into a short black bob with bangs. I had to admit, it looked fantastic. I applied lots of mascara and dramatic red lipstick. *Not bad*, I thought, giving myself one last look in my full-length mirror.

I raced back to Kathy's, and we all admired each other's costumes before helping her put out all the food and light the candles while Donnie started the music with "Monster Mash." People quickly began arriving in all sorts of costumes. Some headed straight for the snacks and drinks while others began dancing to the music.

Anne and Teddy arrived dressed as Frankenstein's monster and his bride. She came over to where I was keeping an eye on the snacks and pouring drinks. "You look fantastic!" she said, speaking loudly to be heard over the music.

"Thanks. So do you." She had somehow managed to make her hair stand straight up.

She laughed. "I'll hate myself later when I'm trying to get all of this goop out of my hair."

"Where'd Teddy go?" I felt like I hadn't seen much of him lately, which was true when I thought about it.

"He's helping Donnie pick out music."

"I should have known." My brother loved music, and he loved it loud, which probably explained why the volume had just gone up.

"What can I do to help?" Anne hollered in my ear.

"Not a thing except maybe keep Teddy from making us all go deaf."

She laughed. "You've got it." She went to pull Teddy onto the dance floor, and Donnie took the opportunity to barely turn the volume down a notch. I guess he liked it loud too.

Kathy came back from schmoozing among her guests to get a drink. "Whew! I should have picked a costume with short sleeves and less hair. Like yours, which is sizzlin', by the way."

I winked at her flirtatiously. "Thanks."

"Have Brian and the wicked witch arrived?"

I laughed. "I don't think so." I scanned the room but stopped when the front door opened again, and grabbed the countertop because my knees had gone wobbly. "Dear God in heaven!"

"What is it?" She followed my gaze. She whistled softly. "You always were a sucker for men in uniform, but I'd have to agree with you on this one."

Brian was walking toward Donnie dressed as a policeman, and I hungrily followed every step of his path with my eyes. The uniform fit in all the right places. I had never noticed his biceps before, but the short sleeves showed them to perfection. I watched them stand out as he shook Donnie's hand. I was practically salivating. And best of all, there was no sign of Delilah.

"Pick up your chin, honey. He's headed this way." Kathy quickly made an exit from behind the counter.

I busied myself rearranging the food platters while seriously trying to regain my composure, looking up only when I heard Brian say, "I'm going to have to ask you to put down that tray of food, ma'am."

"Why is that, Officer?" I asked innocently.

"You're under arrest."

"Arrest? What for?"

"Assault with a deadly weapon." For a second I thought Kathy had told him about my getting the license in the mail, but then he said, "That dress should be illegal."

He'd come around the counter and was fingering my fringe. I could feel the heat rising to my cheeks. "You look pretty hot yourself." I stepped closer and, feeling a little reckless, ran the tip of one finger just under the edge of his sleeve. "Nice blues." I kept my eyes on his badge.

"One of your dad's buddies at the station hooked me up."

I looked up at him, trying to keep my voice casual. "Where's Delilah?"

"She had another conference."

"Already?"

He shrugged. I couldn't tell if he was upset or just disappointed. Before I could figure out what to say, a slow song started, and Brian grabbed my gloved hand. "Come on. Let's dance."

I started to protest because of the food, but Anne had magically arrived at that moment. "I've got it covered, Emma. Go have some fun. You deserve it."

"Don't make me get out the handcuffs," Brian threatened.

"I don't know. That might be kind of fun." What had gotten into me?

Brian smiled and steered me in front of him. I couldn't believe it. I had actually made him blush.

What was it about a man's hand on the small of your back that absolutely sends shockwaves up your spine? I had no idea, but that was exactly what I was experiencing as he guided me onto the floor. He put one arm around my waist and took my hand in his. "Let's show these kids how it's done." He waltzed me around the floor until everyone else had stopped dancing and was watching us. As the song ended, he dipped me, to much applause. I was laughing as he pulled me back up, and we took a bow.

I started to walk away, but he stopped me as another slow song began. This time he placed both of his arms around my waist, leaving me no choice but to put mine around his neck. I saw Kathy beaming next to Donnie, and I knew she had asked him to play another slow one. Bless her heart. I'd thank her later.

Brian had tossed the uniform cap onto the coffee table, and I ruffled his hair where the cap had flattened it. "You owe your mother a thank-you."

"Whatever for?" he asked, smiling down at me.

"For making you take all those dancing lessons. You're a fabulous dancer."

He grimaced. "Man, I hated those lessons. I was afraid all of my friends would call me a sissy."

"Did they?"

"Nah. I threatened to punch their lights out if they did."

"I figured." I slid my arms under his, wrapped them around his waist, and rested my cheek on his chest. I didn't know why we couldn't just stay that way forever.

He rested his chin on the top of my head. "You're such a great friend, Emma. I don't know what I'd do without you."

That's why, I thought as I closed my eyes. *I'm just a friend to him.* I kept silent until the end of the song. Then I excused myself to get a drink.

"You don't have to thank me," Kathy said as I poured myself lemonade. "Things looked awfully cozy out there," Anne teased.

I smiled at them wryly. "He just thinks of me as a friend."

"How do you know?" they asked in unison.

I laughed as they looked at each other. "Because that's what he said just now out on the dance floor. 'You're such a good friend, Emma.' I'm nothing more than that to him." I poured myself another lemonade and grabbed a peanut butter cookie. Ah, comfort food. I took a big bite.

I felt a tap on my shoulder and turned to find a pirate standing beside me. "Would you like to dance?" he asked.

I set my cookie and lemonade aside, considering his offer. *What the heck?* I thought. *I'm here to party, not mope.* "Love to," I said, taking his hand. As we found an empty spot in the center of the room, I noticed that Brian had been snagged by a French maid.

The rest of the evening flew by as I danced with character after character. Brian wasn't lacking for dance partners either, but it was nice to just enjoy myself and get my mind off things.

Finally Donnie called out, "I regret to inform everyone, but this will be that last song of the evening."

The pirate was headed my way, but I suddenly felt cold steel snap around my wrist.

"Sorry, mate," Brian said from behind me, "but this dance is mine." He raised our wrists, which were now handcuffed together.

Laughing, I turned to face Brian as the pirate went to find another partner. "Was it necessary for you to resort to handcuffs just to get a dance with *moi*?"

Brian wiggled his eyebrows. "I was afraid he'd carry you away if I didn't do something drastic."

"Well, I guess you succeeded."

Willie Nelson began singing, "Maybe I didn't love you / Quite as often as I could have," on the stereo as a grinning Brian put his free arm around my waist and clasped our shackled hands together. Willie continued, "Maybe I didn't treat you / Quite as good as I should have." I closed my eyes and listened to the words. "If I made you feel second best / Girl, I'm sorry I was blind."

Crap! Why did Donnie have to play this song for the last dance? "You were always on my mind / You were always on my mind." I was ready to wail my head off at this point.

You can't cry right now, Emma, I thought to myself. *If you start crying, the man you're handcuffed to will not stop asking questions until you blurt everything out.* I started counting candles to distract myself.

The last note of the song faded, and everyone started clapping except for Brian and me. We'd forgotten the handcuffs until we both tried to pull our hands in opposite directions. "I certainly hope you have the key for these," I commented as we headed for the drinks.

"Any particular reason?" He was looking at me strangely.

"Because I've got to go to the little girl's room." I kept walking but almost jerked my arm out of socket when he stopped abruptly. "What's the matter with you?"

"I don't have the key."

"What!" I screeched. People turned to stare as they made their way to the door. I lowered my voice. "How can you not have the key?" I whispered frantically.

"Well, I didn't expect to be using the handcuffs, so I didn't ask for the key."

"This is terrible," I moaned.

"What's terrible?" Kathy asked. Donnie, Teddy, and Anne were standing with her.

I lifted my wrist, pulling Brian's arm up also. "Brian decided to use his handcuffs, but he doesn't have the key."

They all burst out laughing. "Why are you handcuffed at all?" Kathy asked between fits of laughter.

I glared at Brian, who was looking very sheepish. "It's a long story, and it's not funny. We have to get these things off *now*."

"What's your hurry?" Kathy's question sent them into gales of laughter again.

"I've got to go to the bathroom!"

That sobered them. "Have you tried pulling them over your wrists?" This from my ever-practical brother.

"Yes, Teddy." I was trying not to lose my cool. "They're on too tight for that."

"Would it help if we used some butter to make them slippery?" Donnie asked.

"Whatever we try, we'd better hurry," I answered.

We walked to the kitchen, and Kathy smoothed butter over my wrists and under the cuffs. "Okay, I'm going to try to pull it over your wrist. Just don't let me hurt you," she added.

As she pulled, I tried to squish my fingers into the smallest position possible. "Ow! Stop, stop, stop. This isn't working." I grabbed a towel and started wiping the butter off my skin.

"I'm so sorry, Emma. I just didn't think," Brian said.

"It's all right. If I didn't need to pee really badly right now, I'd be laughing my head off too."

"Let me call George and see if he can bring the key over."

"It's after two. We couldn't possibly wake him up for this, and I don't have time to wait." I took a deep breath. "You're just going to have to go to the bathroom with me."

Anne and Kathy couldn't have looked any more horrified than I did. Donnie and Teddy were trying not to laugh again. "Are you sure you don't want me to call George?" Brian asked hopefully.

"Are you kidding?" I started dragging him toward the bathroom. "Not only would I have peed all over myself by the time he got here; it would be all over the station by morning. They'd never let me live it down."

"So what are we going to do?"

"First I'm going to pee. Then I'll figure something out." I came to a halt in front of the toilet, trying to figure out how to handle this particular problem. "Okay, turn around and close your eyes." Wisely, he did as I asked without question. "This is so humiliating," I said under my breath, trying to maneuver my clothing out of the way with one hand.

"Need some help back there?"

"Don't you dare turn around! I've got it handled." I had finally managed to tuck everything up around my waist and sat on the toilet. I tried to pee as quietly as possible, but it sounded extremely loud in the silence of the bathroom. I finished and pulled all my clothing back in place. I pushed the handle down. "You can turn around now."

"Uh, Emma?"

"Yes, Brian?" I was avoiding his eyes.

"I've got to go now."

My head snapped up, and my face got even redder, if that was possible. "Now?" I squeaked.

"Well, hearing you—"

"Stop," I interrupted. "I get it."

We switched places. I heard the sound of Velcro pulling apart. "Could you hold this for a minute?" He handed me his gun belt. "No peeking now," he said. I started giggling. I couldn't help it. I was on the border of hysteria. Giggling quickly became full-out laughter. "You're not helping," he said over his shoulder.

"I'm sorry." I was trying to take deep breaths and not fall on the floor. Luckily my laughter managed to keep me from hearing most of what was going on behind me. After what seemed an eternity, I heard the toilet flush.

"All clear," he said.

We turned to face each other and burst out laughing. I handed him his gun belt. "Don't ever do this to me again," I warned him.

He winced. "Don't worry. I'll never to be able to look at handcuffs the same way again."

We were still laughing when we came out of the bathroom. "Are you guys okay?" Anne asked.

"Yes," we answered in unison.

"What are you going to do?" Kathy asked. "Can't you get a key from someone at the station?"

I thought about it for a minute. "Not an option. I know Dad has some keys at the house, but it's too late to get them tonight. We'll just have to wait until morning and catch him before he goes to church."

"What about tonight?" Brian asked.

"Well, I guess it's either your house or mine. It's not the first time we've slept together." I heard exclamations of surprise and realized what I had just said. "Sorry, that didn't come out right." I started giggling again. It must have been contagious because Kathy and Anne followed suit. The guys just rolled their eyes.

"Your house it is," Brian said after we had gotten ourselves under control again. "You have better food."

Since we wouldn't be much help trying to clean up while stuck together, Brian and I gathered our things and Anne and Teddy stayed instead. We left to much laughter and calls of "sweet dreams." Kathy offered us some of her candles, and I almost throttled her on the spot.

Finally outside, it dawned on us that we had two vehicles there. "Looks like you'll be driving," Brian quipped shaking our cuffed hands. He was right. There was no way he could drive with me shackled to his left side. I stuck my head back through the door. "Teddy, you're going to have to take Brian's car home with you. Just drive it to the parsonage tomorrow morning." I tossed the keys to him. As I closed the door, I heard them burst into laughter again.

We walked to my car, and Brian climbed over the gearshift to the passenger's side. We were in tears from laughing so hard by the time we got to my house. Every time I had to shift gears or turn the wheel, Brian's left hand had had to follow. It was like he had become my shadow.

We stood in the entryway for a minute. "Where first?" he asked.

"I've got to let Mike in and give him his supper."

"Okay. You lead, I'll follow." We walked to the back door where Michelangelo greeted us joyously. I scooped some dog food into his bowl.

"Next?" Brian asked.

"Bed, I guess." We walked to the bedroom and looked at each other uncomfortably. Although we had spent the night together once before, it had been unintentional. We were conscious this time. Suddenly I looked down at my dress. There was no way I was going to be able to take it off.

I think Brian had the same thought. "Do you want to try to get into something else?"

"No. I'll just take off some of the accessories." I took off my wig, shoes, and gloves. Since I was right-handed, I kept jerking his left hand around. "Sorry." Another nervous giggle escaped.

He kicked off his shoes. "No problem." We turned to face the bed. "How are we going to do this?"

I looked at our hands and back at the bed. "I guess I'll sleep on the left and you take the right." I climbed in on the right and slid over to the left, and we finally got everything situated with our handcuffed limbs between us.

"So what's your plan for getting the key tomorrow?" Brian asked. He was yawning already, but I was so wired I didn't think I'd ever get to sleep.

"I'll call Dad first thing tomorrow morning and ask him to bring the key over before going to church."

"How are we ever going to explain this," he shook the cuffs, "much less that we spent the night together?"

"We'll just tell the truth. Dad's an understanding guy."

"I hope so."

Things grew quiet on Brian's side of the bed. I, on the other hand, couldn't get comfortable. I usually slept on my left side, but when I rolled that way, it left my right arm hanging behind me. I rolled onto my back again.

Brian's voice in the dark surprised me. "What are you doing over there?"

"I thought you were asleep."

"Not yet. What's the matter?"

"I can't sleep on my left side. It leaves my arm dangling."

He didn't say anything for a minute. "I have an idea."

"What?"

"Roll this way until your back is to me." I was now on my left side, my head pillowed on his left bicep. "Better?"

"Yes. Thanks. Are you comfortable?"

"I'm fine." I could feel his breath on my neck. "You smell good." He sounded sleepy again. "Like magnolias." I could feel his head move closer to mine on the pillow, and he inhaled deeply.

"It's my lotion."

"Have to tell Delilah about it," he murmured. He wrapped his right arm around my waist and fell asleep.

Chapter Twelve

WHEN I WOKE the next morning, I wasn't exactly sure where I was for a few minutes. Then I saw the glint of sunlight on cold steel around my wrist, and the whole embarrassing situation became perfectly clear. I stayed where I was just enjoying the sight of Brian's face next to mine on the pillow. It was a little early to be calling Dad for the key, so I waited and let Brian sleep. His free hand was resting on my hip and slid around to my stomach when I finally rolled the opposite direction onto my back.

He opened his eyes. "Good morning, sunshine." His uniform was a little rumpled, but it still looked pretty good. I looked down at my dress. I didn't think the fringe would ever be the same.

"Morning, Officer. Sleep all right?"

"Like a baby. You?"

"Not bad." I rose up on one arm and looked over his shoulder to see the clock. It was eight. "Hand me the phone, will you? Might as well call Dad and see if he has a key."

Brian handed me the phone, and I dialed the number. "Hello?" Crap! Mother had answered the phone.

"Hello, Mother. Is Dad there?" I kept my tone as neutral as possible.

"What do you need Dad for?"

"Nothing. I just need to ask him something."

"Something you can't ask me?" she asked haughtily.

I sighed. "Let's just say it's his area of expertise. Is he there or not?"

"I think he's already walked over to the church."

"Could you check to be sure?"

"Just a minute." I listened to silence for several minutes. "He's already left, Emma. Is it something I can help you with?"

"No, that's okay. I'll just call him in his office. 'Bye."

I hung up before she could ask any more questions. Brian looked at me in amusement. "You just made her curious, didn't you?"

"Yes." I dialed the number for Dad's office at the church. "Dad? It's Emma."

"Well, good morning, sweetheart. Did you get some rest? I wouldn't want you to fall asleep again," he teased.

"Some, Dad. I have a favor to ask. Do you still have your old handcuff keys?"

"Yes. Why?"

"Because I need one."

"Why do you need a handcuff key?" he asked in surprise.

"It's a long story. I hate to ask, but could you get them and bring them to my house?"

"Emma, what is going on?"

"Please, Dad. I'll explain it when you get here."

He sighed. "Okay. I'll be there in a few minutes."

I hung up and looked at Brian. "He'll be here in a few minutes."

"I guess we should get up then."

"That's probably a good idea." I slid over to his side of the bed, and he grabbed my hands to help me up. We let

Michelangelo outside and went into the kitchen to start the coffee and toast some bagels. I needed to use the bathroom again, but I was determined to hold it until the cuffs were off.

"I bet you're wishing you were left-handed right about now." Brian was laughing at my efforts.

"It's easier to try it this way than having to lift the weight of your arm every time I take a sip or bite. Don't think I didn't notice that you shackled your left hand." I lifted it with mine and shook them at him.

"It wasn't a conscious decision," he protested. "I just grabbed the cuffs with my right and slapped them on my left."

The doorbell rang. "Thank goodness. Help is here." I waited for Brian to put down his coffee cup before dragging him to the door and opening it. "Dad, I'm so glad you're—" Mother was standing beside him.

"Why do you need a handcuff key, Emma, and why are you dressed like that?" Mother was being her normal nosy self.

Dad looked sheepish. "I'm sorry, Emma. I had to go back to the parsonage for the key, and she wheedled the story out of me. She insisted on coming."

"And why shouldn't I?" Mother demanded sharply. "She's my daughter too."

I felt Brian give my cuffed hand a little squeeze with his behind the door, and I stepped aside to let them into the house, where they finally saw Brian. Before they could react, I stuck out our cuffed hands. "Please just undo this."

Dad started cackling while he dug the key from his pocket. "I should have known something like this was going to happen when Larry lent you a uniform," he said to Brian, who looked relieved that Dad wasn't upset.

Mother, however, looked horrified. "How long have you two been shackled together?"

I looked her in the eye. "Since yesterday evening at the costume party."

"All night?"

Brian answered quickly. "Yes, but nothing happened, Mrs. Bailey."

"Now, Brian," I said coyly. "Let's tell the truth." Mother's self-righteous displeasure was beginning to irk me. Dad stopped fiddling with the handcuffs. "I spent the entire evening snuggled up in this man's arms. In my bed. While handcuffed to him." Mother gave a little gasp and covered her mouth. "We were fully clothed, Mother. Jeez! Look at us. Do you really think I was doing the deed like this with Brian?" I was going to have to spend considerable time praying about the images that statement had just conjured in my head.

"Oh, dear. Whatever will people say?" she asked. Dad just laughed again and went back to working on the hand-cuffs, shaking his head.

"They're going to say nothing because they're going to know nothing as long as we all keep our mouths shut." I looked at her pointedly.

"Well, I certainly won't be shouting this to the hills," she said.

"Free again!" Dad held up the handcuffs, smiling.

Brian rubbed his wrist. "Thank you, Mr. Bailey."

"No problem, son. Let's just not make this a habit with my daughter." He winked. "Unless you keep a key nearby. You know what? Why don't you keep this one just in case?"

"Dad!" My face was as red as my dress. "Thank you for this, but I think you and Mother should be getting back to church. I'll be there as soon as I can get suitably attired."

Dad grinned at Brian. "Son, why don't you join us for dinner? You can tell us how all this happened. I know I enjoy a good story."

"Thank you, Mr. Bailey. I will."

Mother was still looking askance at the whole situation.

"Come on, Evelyn," Dad said. "Let the kids get ready for church. See y'all in a little while."

As the door shut behind them, Brian turned to me. "Your mother didn't look happy."

I pointed my finger at him. "You better make the story really good at lunch, or we're toast for a while."

"Your dad certainly got a kick out of it." He chuckled.

"I guarantee you he's on his way to the phone to tell every single one of his buddies about it. It'll be all over town before the service is over because they'll have to tell their wives, who'll tell their friends, so on and so forth."

"You have nothing to be ashamed about."

"You know that, and I know that, but that's not how it will get portrayed."

"Let the old bats say what they will. We'll just ignore them."

"I wish it were that easy," I said under my breath.

"Well, I had a good time last night anyway." One of my straps had fallen off my shoulder, and he slid it back into place. It was almost like a caress.

I wanted to tangle my fingers in his hair and kiss him like crazy, but I turned and gave him a hug instead. "So did I.

We better get cleaned up for church. Just come over when you're ready to go."

"All right. See you in a few."

Exactly thirty minutes later, I heard him call from the living room, "Are you decent?"

"Yeah."

He stuck his head into the bathroom where I was in my bathrobe preparing to put lotion on my legs. "Why does it take y'all so long to get ready?"

I made a face at him in the mirror. "Because we women have a lot more that we have to do. Guys don't have to wear makeup, shave their legs, curl their hair, etc."

"Mind if I watch and learn?" He sat on the edge of the tub.

"Be my guest." Feeling a little wicked, I decided to put on a little show before church. I'd deal with my conscience later. I propped one leg on the toilet, pulling my bathrobe up to expose it without showing anything else.

"What are you doing?" He looked a little uncomfortable.

"Just putting lotion on my legs," I said innocently. I reached for the magnolia-scented lotion that he liked so much, although his comment last night about Delilah still stung. I squirted a line of the lotion up my leg and began to massage it into my skin slowly. Leaning forward to rub some lotion on my foot, I let one sleeve of my bathrobe fall off my shoulder, giving him a little glimpse of cleavage before demurely pulling it back up again. Then I snuck a peek at him. He was trying hard to look everywhere but at me. I smiled because he wasn't succeeding.

I propped my other foot up and teased the bathrobe open to the top of my leg again. Another line of lotion.

Another slow massage of the leg. I closed the lotion bottle and stood all the way up. The top of my bathrobe had fallen open a little again, but I pretended not to notice.

Immediately he was standing right beside me. I turned to face him, and he grasped the collar of my bathrobe gently. My pulse accelerated as he stood there for a moment. The he pulled the sides of the robe together and tightened the belt. "So what are you going to wear?" He walked toward the closet.

Well, he had noticed, so he wasn't completely immune to me as a woman. I decided to up the ante a little. I walked to the dresser and dug through one of the drawers. "Oh, I don't know. Which do you think?" I turned to look at him. In one hand, I held a matching black satin bra, panties, and garter belt set. In the other hand, I held the same set in red satin. I'd never worn either, but a girl never knew when she might need something like this. He was blushing. I smiled. "Red it is." I put the black set back in the drawer and threw the red set on the bed.

He had turned back to the closet. "Uh. I think you should wear this." He had picked a high-necked, long-sleeved dress that I didn't even know I had in my closet.

"That old thing? It's ugly." I searched through my clothes. "How about this?" I pulled a solid black wrap dress from the hanger. Because it was held together by only two little ties, the wrap dress was v-necked without being obscene, and the skirt inevitably would split to show a little leg. I selected a pair of black heels from the shoe rack.

"Isn't that a little drab for church?"

"It's perfect. I'll just be a second." I set the heels by the bed and grabbed my underwear off the bed before shutting myself in the bathroom to dress. When I walked back into the bedroom, Brian was sitting on the bed. I struck a pose.

"What do you think?"

He smiled a little. "You're beautiful as always."

"Thanks, and I'm not even through yet." I walked over to the dresser and dug through another drawer for nude stockings.

"You're not?"

"Nope. I've still got to put on my makeup."

"You don't really need it, you know."

That stopped me cold. "I don't?"

"I think you're just as pretty now as you are when you have it on."

I looked at him in astonishment. His eyes showed his sincerity. "Thank you, Brian. That's about the nicest compliment a girl can get." I took the stockings over to the bed and sat down beside him.

"Those aren't normal pantyhose."

"No, they're not. These are stockings. Let me demonstrate." I pulled on the first stocking and opened the split of my skirt just enough to fasten the straps of the garter belt. "See? The garter belt holds them up." He nodded his head mutely. I put on the other stocking and hitched the other side of my skirt so I could fasten those straps. This was too much fun! I pulled on my heels and gave his leg a pat as I stood up to head for the bathroom.

He grabbed my hand and stopped me. I turned to face him. "What is it?" He didn't say a word, but he pulled my left leg up and propped my foot on the bed where he was sitting. The skirt of my dress split to show the tops of my stockings and the red straps of the garter belt. My breath caught in my throat, and I put a hand on his shoulder to balance myself. "What are you doing?"

He slid a finger under a strap and down to where it met the stocking. I thought my heart was going to beat out of my chest. He said, "I just wanted to see up close how it hooked to the stocking."

"Oh." I almost fainted when he slid his hands down my leg to set my foot back down on the floor. I definitely was not immune to him as a man. I turned and walked to the bathroom where I quickly applied mascara, blush, and lip gloss. No need to apply a lot if he thought I looked good without it.

He was still sitting on the bed when I came out of the bathroom. "Hair up or down?" I asked.

He looked at me blankly for a second. "Definitely down."

I tied a red scarf around my neck. Just a little reminder of what I was wearing underneath the dress. "Well, I'm ready."

As we entered the back of the sanctuary, everything became very quiet. "Looks like everybody's heard," Brian whispered. "Let them talk." He took my hand in his and walked to our pew. Gradually the whispering started again behind us. Steve was standing in the aisle straight ahead, and he was watching us closely.

"Well, you seem to be having a good time this morning," he commented as we approached our pew.

"It's a lovely morning," I replied. "You know me; give me a sunny day, and I'm happy as a lark." I moved into the pew, and Steve stepped in front of Brian to sit beside me. After we sat down with Steve very close beside me, Brian stepped around us and sat on my other side. Despite feeling like I was in the middle of some bizarre grade school rivalry, I scooted a little closer to Brian in order to give myself some breathing room.

Mother had refrained from making her customary trips across the aisle this morning and was sitting in our pew staring stonily ahead. "Good morning, Mrs. Bailey," Brian greeted her as we sat down. She simply nodded. Brian put his arm behind me on the back of the pew and leaned to whisper into my ear. "Looks like her mood has deteriorated even further."

"I'm sure one of the old bats cornered her when she got to church," I whispered back. "I ought to kill Dad." Steve was getting closer to me on the pew, trying to hear what we were saying. I turned to give him a very pointed look, and he scooted back.

Brian leaned over to whisper in my ear. "Don't be too hard on him." He was playing with the end of my scarf. "If it wasn't for him, we'd still be cuffed together in our costumes."

I turned toward him slightly and casually put my hand on his knee, smiling up at him. "It turned out to be kind of fun. Made me appreciate my dominant hand." I gave his leg a pat with said hand. I could almost feel the heat from Steve's angry glares on the back of my head.

Brian grinned. "And I got to learn why women take so long to get ready." I felt a snap against my leg and looked down to find that the skirt of my dress had split open a little to reveal one of my garter straps, which he had just gleefully popped against my leg.

I carefully closed the opening in my skirt and tucked it under me while playfully slapping his hand away. "Behave yourself."

Someone cleared their throat behind me, and we looked up to find a grinning Anne and Teddy, who had just witnessed that last scene. I think I blushed from the tips of my toes to the top of my head. "For a minute there," Teddy murmured, "I thought the two of you were still cuffed."

Brian laughed as we made room for them to sit next to us. Anne raised an eyebrow. I winked at her and mouthed, "Tell you later."

"Handcuffs?" Steve asked suspiciously.

"Long story," I whispered as Dad stepped into the pulpit. I didn't hear much of the sermon because I was too distracted by Brian's nearness and his playing with my scarf. It tickled my neck every time he pulled on the end of it. Steve just glowered.

Anne and I walked ahead of the guys to the parsonage after the service had ended. "What was going on between you and Brian back there?" she demanded.

"Just a little payback." I told her about the morning's "lessons."

"Emma, you're terrible." She was giggling.

"I know, but it was so much fun to make him remember that I was a woman as well as his friend!" I quickly lowered my voice again. "I suspect he's been trying to turn the tables on me, but I plan to come out on top." Anne burst out laughing, and I gave her a little jab with my elbow. "You know what I meant."

"What do you have up your sleeve now?"

"Watch and see."

I headed straight for the bathroom to reapply my lip gloss and fluff my curls a little. Then I tightened my bra a couple of notches. A little more cleavage wouldn't hurt now that we were out of church. Finally I pulled the scarf from around my neck and tied it around my waist. I certainly didn't want it to end up in my plate.

Steve cornered me outside the bathroom. "What's going on between you and Brian?" he demanded.

"What do you mean?"

He frowned. "You'd think you two were dating, as much time as you spend together and especially after the way you were acting this morning."

"Well, we're not. I'm a spinster, remember. We're just friends."

He took a deep breath and exhaled. "Okay, then let's do something together this afternoon."

I shook my head. "I'm sorry, Steve, but I already have plans with Brian." We hadn't said anything definite, but I was going to assume we had. "We needed some time to catch up on each other's lives, and he's got a free afternoon since his girlfriend is out of town." I almost choked on the word.

"Fine. Why don't you give me a call when you have time for *this* friend?" He grabbed his car keys and stalked to the door. He stopped and glared down the hallway toward the dining room. "He's going to wish he'd never met me." The door slammed behind him.

I didn't like the sound of that, but there wasn't anything I could do about it now. I'd try to talk to him later. I joined Anne and Mother in the kitchen. Anne took one look at me and quickly turned back to stirring a pot on the stove, but not before I saw her grin.

"What can I do, Mother?"

"Would you slice the cucumbers?" she asked, her tone chilly.

"Sure." I grabbed a knife from the stand and started slicing. Brian came into the kitchen with Teddy and stopped next to me. He grabbed a cucumber slice, and I slapped his hand. "Stop it. You'll ruin your dinner."

He grabbed another one and stood behind me. I kept slicing, trying to ignore him, but he leaned over my shoulder and said, "There's one advantage to being tall."

"Just one? What's that?" I replied.

"I have a great view from wherever I stand." I quit slicing as he grabbed another cucumber and planted a kiss on my check. "Thanks for the appetizers," he called as he and Teddy left the kitchen.

I snuck a glance over my shoulder as I started slicing again. Mother looked puzzled, Anne was laughing over her pot, and I was overheated. I walked over to the refrigerator to fill glasses with ice and to cool myself off.

Dinner didn't go quite as I had planned. Although I sat next to Brian and did my best to keep his attention focused on me, it didn't work. First, he had to smooth Mother's rumpled feathers over our having spent the night handcuffed together, and he succeeded as always, but then Teddy engaged him in a long conversation about sports. No one could get a word in edgewise.

I had envisioned Brian and me spending a quiet evening together curled up on the couch and watching a movie, but it wasn't to be. Delilah had called while we were washing the dishes, and Brian had gone running to meet her. I left shortly after that to spend yet another quiet evening at home with Michelangelo.

The next morning Kathy insisted on a detailed version of the weekend's events after Brian and I had left the party.

I thought she would never quit laughing about Brian's lofty view. "You go, girl!" was all that she could finally get out.

Thanks to a mad rush of early Christmas shoppers, the next few days flew by quickly. After seeing the success of the few days since Halloween, we decided to open the store on Saturdays as well during the holiday shopping season.

I couldn't believe it was already Friday. I hadn't seen or heard from Brian since Sunday afternoon. Obviously I hadn't made enough of an impression on him to break the spell of Delilah's charms. Steve had apparently fallen off the face of the earth as well, which didn't bother me much except for his parting comment on Sunday. I was a little worried that he might be trying to plot some kind of revenge against Brian, but I couldn't imagine what it would be. John had sent me an e-mail letting me know that his mother was doing much better. Business was booming and keeping him busy, but he hoped to see me in a few weeks.

I left the store at half past five and had just dressed in yoga pants and a sports bra to work off some steam with Pilates when the doorbell rang. Brian was standing there with a DVD in his hand.

"Well, hello, stranger." I stepped back to let him inside. "Where have you been all week?"

His eyes bounced all over the place trying to avoid my sports bra and bare midriff. They finally settled on Michelangelo. He walked over to scratch the dog's ears. "Just keeping busy. How's your week been?"

"Same old stuff."

"Well, I've got something to cheer you up this evening. I found a Cary Grant movie that we can both enjoy." He held the DVD out to me. "*North by Northwest*."

"What makes you think I need cheering up? Are you saying you haven't enjoyed the other Cary Grant movies we've watched in the past?" I was irritated now. "Don't feel obligated to watch movies that you don't like for my sake, Brian. I'm not some whining baby that needs a pacifier."

"Well, it sure seems to work most of the time," he retorted.

So that's what he thought of me. Pain cut through my heart as I walked to the door and opened it. "I'm afraid I don't have time for Cary or you tonight." I walked back to my yoga mat and sat on it. "Please shut the door behind you on your way out."

I started my Pilates as he stomped toward the door. He paused halfway and turned as if to say something, but I closed my eyes and continued my exercises until I heard the door shut behind him. Then I let my arms and legs fall to the floor, trying to understand what had just happened.

Although he hadn't spoken to me all week, he'd come over here expecting me to be depressed over something and in need of cheering up. Did he think my life so predictably awful? There was only one answer. He pitied me.

I desperately wanted a pint of chocolate ice cream, but that was becoming a very bad habit with me. I did an hour of Pilates instead and had a long soak in the tub before going to bed.

Hours later, I got tired of tossing and turning, so I went to the bookstore. If I couldn't sleep, I could at least keep busy. I took all of the books off the shelves and dusted everything. Then I wiped down the books and rearranged them into new sections. I was putting the final book back on the shelf when Kathy walked through the door.

"Wow!" she exclaimed. "This place is sparkling. How long have you been here?"

"A while." I blew a stray curl out of my eyes.

She looked at me closely. "You've been here all night, haven't you?"

I shrugged as I walked toward the front counter. "Pretty close."

"What happened, Emma?"

I told her about Brian's comments as I started polishing the counter. "I'm sure he didn't mean it," Kathy said when I'd finished. "Delilah's probably just got his pants in a snitch."

"Well, he'll never be able to say it about me again. I'm moving on."

"What do you mean?"

I felt something harden inside me as I said it. "I'm done with all of them. Men are more headache than they're worth."

Kathy looked disconcerted. "Now, honey, you're hurt. You shouldn't make drastic decisions when you're upset."

"It's not a drastic decision. There's no reason to live my life moping around. I'll show him."

"Something had to have been wrong with Brian because there's no way he would have said something like that if he'd been himself."

I shook my head. "I'm not sure I know who the real Brian is anymore."

The next two weeks were terrible. I barely saw Brian, much less tried to talk to him. I suspected his girlfriend was keeping him busy. He'd brought Delilah to church the last two Sundays, and I had been as sweet as honey to her. Brian could have no complaints about my behavior in that respect.

To make matters worse, Thanksgiving was this Thursday, which meant hours cooped up with the family making horrendous jokes about my being single. I went to work on Tuesday morning in a foul mood.

I slammed my purse onto the counter. "I cannot believe my mother."

"What'd she do this time?" Kathy asked as she retrieved more bags from the storeroom.

"She had the gall to call me last night and tell me that I needed to bring someone to Thanksgiving so that I wouldn't be the only single person there."

"You're kidding."

"I'm not. She even named all the couples to prove her point."

"So are you going to bring someone?" Kathy asked hesitantly.

"No. My decision to give up on dating may have been a rash outburst in the beginning, but I mean it now. I told her I wasn't going to bring someone just to make her guest list an even number and that she just had to deal with it."

"How'd she take that?"

"She slammed the phone in my ear."

"Should be a fun day."

"At least it's only half a day. I'm going to the Davises' that evening."

Kathy looked up. "You're going to spend the evening at Brian's parents' house?"

I shrugged. "They invited me, and his mom will be hurt if I don't come. I can't hurt her too."

She looked perplexed. "But I thought that you and Brian…"

I shrugged. "We're still...I don't...I'll need somewhere to escape to after spending half the day with my family."

"True," she said.

I decided to turn the conversation away from my problems. "What are you going to do for Thanksgiving?"

Her faced erupted into a huge grin. "Donnie is taking me to meet his family."

"Really? That's great, Kathy." I gave her a huge hug.

"I think so, but I'm a nervous wreck." She was wringing her hands.

I grabbed them tightly. "Don't be. They can't help but love you like we all do."

"Thanks, Emma." Her smile was radiant.

Brian's mom called me that night to make sure I was still coming. "Brian said y'all had a misunderstanding."

"You could say that, but I will be there anyway."

"You do that, and you can tell me all about it when you get here." The welcome in her voice made me feel better. "Bring some clothes and Michelangelo too so you can stay over. I have a big turkey leg with his name on it."

"Are you sure?"

"Absolutely. I want to keep you as long as possible, and that dog of yours is a darling."

Chapter Thirteen

THANKSGIVING MORNING DAWNED unseasonably warm for this time of year. I wouldn't have to worry about leaving Michelangelo in the backyard. He was already plopped in the grass enjoying the warmth from the sun. I packed up my pumpkin roll and headed to the parsonage.

Uncle Richard pounced as soon as I opened the door. "Alone again this year, eh, Emma?" He threw a beefy arm around my shoulder and propelled me into the living room where all the men in the family were watching football. "Well, Ted, looks like you're going to have to use the turkey baster on this one if you want to get any grandchildren from her." I wanted to strangle him as they all started laughing.

Dad gave a big laugh and answered, "I've been talking to the guys at the precinct about that. I suggested they offer a free pass out of jail to some of the perps if they'll donate a sample to the cause." Another round of raucous laughter whirled around the room as I hid my disgust behind a smile and hurried to the kitchen for escape—or so I thought.

I saw Anne up to her elbows in stuffing. She threw me a sympathetic look as Aunt Hattie took my pumpkin roll out of my hands. "Emma, your mother tells me you're still single. What's the matter? Do you scare 'em all off? You're not getting any younger, darlin'. You better catch yourself a husband soon, or you'll be an old maid. I could give you some pointers if you like." Aunt Hattie had just gotten married to husband number four.

"No thanks. In case you hadn't heard, I've already chosen to be an old maid. Quite happily in fact." She looked at me in disbelief before making a beeline for Mother.

I went to the backyard only to be accosted by Aunt May. "Emma, you know you could tell us if you were a...well... you know what," she whispered. She was obviously uncomfortable with saying the word lesbian.

"I'm not, Aunt May. I just haven't found a man with the stamina to keep up with my sexual appetite," I answered sweetly.

"Oh." She quickly turned away to go back into the house.

The comments and jokes only got worse as I made the rounds through the rest of the family. I finally took refuge in the bathroom to get a few minutes' peace until dinner was served.

"Emma, would you mind sitting at the head of the children's table and keeping an eye on things there?" Mother asked. "We only have an even number of chairs at the adult table, and there's no sense in splitting up any of the couples since you're here alone."

So that was my punishment for telling her to deal with it. "No problem, Mother. I'd be happy to do that for you." I'd eat fast and make my escape to the Davises' more quickly that way.

We all took our places at the tables, and Dad said the blessing. Everyone quickly filled their plates and started eating. The conversation around the table was quite clearly about me and my "attitude" as Mother called it. They clearly thought it was just a bitter phase.

As the desserts were going around, Teddy stood and tapped his water glass with his spoon. "May I have everyone's attention please? Anne and I have an announcement." Anne stood proudly beside him, and I knew exactly what was coming. "Another little Bailey will be joining us in June of next year!"

Mother and Dad jumped up to embrace the beaming couple, and everyone was shouting their congratulations.

"Looks like your younger brother beat you again, Emma," Uncle Richard boomed over the noise. I had a split second to get a smile on my face before everyone turned to stare.

"Yes, he did, Uncle Richard. I always suspected he would."

Everyone finally turned back to their desserts, but mine lay untouched on my plate. I was envious of my brother and my friend, and I hated myself for it. I said my good-byes as everyone left the tables.

"But you've only been here a few hours," Mother protested.

"Yes, but I was also invited to the Davises', and it's a two-hour drive from here. I want to get there before dark."

"Fine," she said, taking a stack of dishes to the kitchen.

I went to retrieve my purse from one of the bedrooms. Anne had followed me. "Emma, are you all right?"

"I'm fine. Why wouldn't I be?"

"I know everyone's been giving you a hard time today, and you just seemed to get very quiet after our news. I was afraid you were upset."

I gave her a hug. "I'm just tired. I'm happy for you, Anne. Truly, I am. After all, I'm going to be an auntie."

She gave me another hug. "Drive carefully."

"I will." A guardian angel must have been watching over me because I managed to get out of the house quietly without anymore of Uncle Richard's tacky comments.

After grabbing my bag at the house and getting Michelangelo loaded into the car, I finally arrived at the Davises' at five o'clock. Mr. Davis greeted me at the door with a boisterous bear hug and sent me into the living room while he took care of my bag and Michelangelo.

Brian's two brothers, Andrew and Peter, stood as I entered the room. "There's our adopted sister!" Andrew greeted me with a hug much like his dad's.

"Hello, Andrew." I turned to Peter and gave him a hug. "How are you, Petey?"

"Darling, I couldn't be better, and you couldn't be any prettier." He leaned down and whispered into my ear, "When is that brother of mine going to wise up and marry you?"

I blinked away the tears that quickly sprang to my eyes and whispered back jokingly, "From your lips to God's ears."

I greeted their wives and Brian's two sisters, Mary and Grace, who were also there with their spouses. The grandchildren were everywhere, but Brian was nowhere to be seen.

My disappointment must have shown. As she took me in her arms, Mom said, "He left shortly before you got here to go to that Delilah woman's house, but I'm so glad you're here, dear. We'll talk a little later, just the two of us."

We spent the next few hours catching up on everyone's lives and how the kids were doing in school. I never had to worry about them harassing me about my being single, and it was a nice change. As we chatted, the stress that had built from earlier in the day melted away from me. I was yawning before the kids were.

"Come on, dear. Let's get you to bed. You're about to drop where you're sitting," Mom said as she took my hand and pulled me off the couch.

"I'm sorry, y'all." I yawned again. "I guess the day's just catching up with me."

"You go get some rest, Emma." Mr. Davis gave me another hug. "We'll all be here tomorrow."

They all said good night, and Mom led me up the stairs to Brian's room. "All the other rooms are taken, but Brian said he'd stay at his place tonight instead of making the drive back, so you'll be all right in here. She sat down on the bed and pulled me down beside her. "Now tell me about this misunderstanding."

I rubbed my eyes. "It's no misunderstanding. He made it perfectly clear how he feels about me."

"What do you mean?"

I told her every detail of the whole horrible scene. "I've become a nuisance and a bore to him." My bottom lip was beginning to tremble against my will.

Mom shook her head slowly. "I don't know what to think of that boy since that Delilah woman's come along, but, Emma, I know he couldn't have meant what he said."

"I don't know, Mom. Things haven't been the same since. I haven't seen him without Delilah once, and we've barely spoken to each other."

"You definitely need to talk to each other. It's the only way you're going to work anything out." She smiled slightly. "Maybe things will be different tomorrow."

I gave her a halfhearted smile. "I hope so."

She gave me another hug. "Good night, dear. Just holler if you need anything."

I changed into my green satin nightgown and laid the matching robe at the end of the bed. I slid under the covers and laid my head on Brian's pillow. For once, I quickly fell asleep.

❧

I awoke to the touch of bare skin against my arm. Forgetting where I was, I took a deep breath to scream, but a hand clamped over my mouth. I struggled to free myself until the light blinded me from the bedside lamp. A bare-chested Brian was sitting on the side of the bed. He removed his hand from my mouth. "What the heck are you doing here, Emma?" he whispered.

"Nice to see you too, Brian. I was invited, remember?" My heart was still pounding, and I was trying to get my breathing back to normal.

"I mean, what are you doing in my room?" His eyes had drifted below my face.

I looked down to see that parts of me had responded to the chill in the room and maybe something else. I quickly snatched the covers back up to my chin. "This is where your mother put me. What are you doing here? She said you were going to spend the night at your place."

He looked surprised. "I never told her that. I said I'd be back tonight, but it would be late."

I sat there staring at him trying to figure out how she could have forgotten that he was coming back tonight. A light bulb went off in my head. She'd done it on purpose so that we would have to talk to each other. "I guess she forgot," I said, knowing very well that she hadn't.

"That's odd." He stood, and I realized he was in nothing but his boxers. I watched his body in the lamplight as he bent to retrieve his clothes. His muscles flexed and stretched with every movement. He was breathtaking. I was startled when he spoke again. "You stay here, and I'll go sleep on the couch."

"No. That's not necessary, Brian. We've slept in the same bed before. This isn't any different."

"You're sure?"

I nodded, and he let his clothes fall back to the floor. I slid over to the other side of the bed as he got under the covers. "So how was Thanksgiving at Delilah's?"

"It was great. How were things at your family's house?"

"Wonderful. Couldn't have been better," I gushed.

He was looking at me. "You're lying."

"Well, at least I'm not whining," I said quietly and rolled away from him.

I felt his hand on my shoulder. "Emma, look at me." I didn't move. "Emma, I said look at me." I refused to budge. Next thing I knew, he'd pulled me to the middle of the bed and was pinning me down so I couldn't get away. I closed my eyes tightly.

"Emma, open your eyes and look at me, or I'm going to start tickling."

I opened my eyes and look up into his face only inches from mine. He knew he'd hurt me deeply. "Babe, I'm sorry. I'd take back every bit of it if I could. I don't know why I said it. I didn't mean it." His face grew blurry as the tears came and fell back into my hair. I closed my eyes again as he rested his forehead on mine for a moment. "I'm so sorry."

He lay back on his pillow turning off the lamp and pulling me into his arms. As my head rested on his chest, I could feel his hand stroking my back until my tears subsided. "Now," he said into the darkness. "Tell me how it really went today." He was playing with my hair.

"Anne's having a baby."

"That's great."

"It is."

"But?" I felt his lips against my hair and snuggled closer.

"But I wasn't happy at the news. I envied them."

"Because?"

"Because I wanted it to be me."

"It will be you someday, Emma."

"I don't think so, Brian."

"Well, there's no doubt in my mind. Some guy's going to carry you off one of these days regardless of what you've said in the past. I just hope he deserves you," he added quietly. I drifted off to sleep as his fingers coiled in my hair.

❦

"Well, well, well. What do we have here?" I recognized the voice, but my brain couldn't put a name with it.

"Ah, shut up, Andrew." That was Brian. Brian was talking to Andrew. "It's all Mom's doing." *What was Mom's doing?* I moved a little and felt an arm tighten around me. "She put Emma in my bed, and I didn't know it." I was in Brian's bed?

"Looks like you know it now."

I moved again and felt bare skin beneath my cheek. "Be quiet. You're going to wake her." I heard a door close, and I opened one eye. Brian was grinning at me.

"Good morning, sleepyhead."

"Good morning." I was still lying on his chest, and one of my legs had gotten wrapped around his.

"Andrew came to say good morning, but you were still asleep."

My eyes flew open, and I looked up at him in horror. "Andrew was in here?" I looked at how I was lying across him and quickly sat up. "And saw us like that?"

"It's no big deal."

"No big deal! What will he think? What will your mother think when he tells her?" I scrambled out of bed and pulled on my robe.

He calmly got out of bed and walked to where I was frantically pulling clothes out of my bag. "Emma." I kept digging. "Emma." He took my arms in his hands and looked me in the eyes. "I promise they won't think anything bad. In fact, I think my darling mom set us up."

"You do?"

"Yes, I do. She's tried to get me to talk to you for the last two weeks. I think this was her way of forcing the issue."

"So do I." I gave him a small smile and turned back to my bag.

"Get a move on." I felt a sharp slap on my behind. "It's time for breakfast."

I threw my shoe at him as he sauntered over to pick up his clothes. It missed. "What was that for?" he asked, surprised.

"You slapped my butt." I walked over to retrieve my shoe.

"It was just a pat of affection."

"Like this?" I pinched his as he bent over to pull up his jeans.

"You're in trouble now," he said as he zipped them up. "I didn't pinch." He began stalking me around the bed.

I was giggling. "Brian, I've got to get dressed."

"You should have thought of that before."

I tried to get around him, but he grabbed me and fell back with me on the bed. I managed to sit on his waist and grabbed his hands, but it did no good. He rolled me over on my back and pinned my arms above my head with one of his. I wrapped my legs around his waist, although it didn't accomplish anything. He trailed his free hand down my cheek and neck, across my collarbone, and down my side, pausing at my rib cage.

My skin jumped everywhere he touched it. "Please don't tickle me," I begged, quietly holding his eyes with mine. He released my arms and started to roll away from me, but I wrapped my arms around his neck. It would be so easy to just kiss him. He looked at me in surprise, and it seemed as if everything was moving in slow motion as he slid his hands beneath my head and back, then sat up, pulling me with him, my legs and arms still wrapped around him. I smiled as his hands slid to the small of my back, pulling me closer to him. His eyes strayed to my mouth. I desperately wanted him to kiss me, and I closed my eyes as his hands slid back up into my hair. These weren't the actions of a friend; they were the actions of a lover. This was promising. I opened my eyes to see his face just an inch from mine.

The spell was broken by a knock at the door. "Brian, breakfast is ready," Andrew called through the door.

"Be right there," Brian yelled back. He was breathing shallowly and looking at me in glassy-eyed horror.

Embarrassed, I unwrapped myself from him and went back to my clothes. He finished getting dressed without another word and left the room. I finished dressing and hurried down to breakfast after making a quick stop in the bathroom to brush my teeth and pull my curls into a ponytail.

Brian and I endured much good-natured teasing about our ending up in the same bed the night before, but everyone was quickly distracted by the food. Mom had made her famous cocoa gravy and biscuits again. I had been skeptical of the idea of chocolate gravy the first time I saw it, but after one bite, I was hooked.

After breakfast, I checked on Michelangelo with Alissa. She was Mary's youngest at three years old, and she had latched onto me. She was adorable, especially when she spoke because she couldn't pronounce some consonants. Michelangelo was happily chewing the turkey leg that Mom had given him, so we left him alone and followed the others to the stables where we petted the horses and fed them apples. Then we all loaded into a horse-drawn wagon to go find a Christmas tree somewhere on the ranch. I had the feeling that Brian was trying to avoid me.

When we reached the grove of cedar trees, everyone spread out to find the best one. After much discussion, we finally settled on one, and the men went to work sawing it down. Once it was loaded into the back of the wagon, we headed back to the house where Mom had reheated the turkey and all of its trimmings. Thanksgiving leftovers were always better the next day.

We stuffed our bellies full, and then the guys brought the tree into the house. We spent the rest of the afternoon stringing popcorn and hanging ornaments while the grandkids made new ones. We were a noisy bunch, everybody laughing and talking at the same time, but before long, the tree was decorated, and we all sat our weary bodies on the couch with the kids sitting around the tree and staring at the twinkling lights.

Mom sat down at the piano and began to play Christmas carols. As we all sang along, I looked around at all the smiling couples and families. Husbands had their arms around their wives or held their hands. I glanced briefly at Brian on the couch opposite me before turning back to watch Mom play. He'd been pretty quiet this evening, and it was no longer just a feeling. He was definitely avoiding me.

Mom began playing "The Christmas Waltz," and I closed my eyes to block out the scene around me. Suddenly someone grabbed my hand. I looked up and saw Brian standing over me. "May I have this dance?" he asked.

"Sure." I was surprised but let him pull me off the couch, and everyone watched as he twirled me faster and faster around the room until I was breathless with laughter. Mom ended the song with a flourish, and he gave me one final twirl.

"Uh-oh. You two stopped under the mistletoe," Andrew called out over the applause. "Kiss her, Brian."

Sure enough, it was directly above us. I looked back at Brian, wondering how we were going to get out of this. "Kiss her, you idiot," Petey added.

He leaned down quickly and pecked my cheek. "That's not a kiss," Mr. Davis' voice boomed above the *boos*. "Try again, and do it right this time."

Brian looked at everyone and turned back to me, smiling. I wasn't sure what to expect. He lifted my arms around his neck and put his around my waist, pulling me close as his brothers hooted and hollered. He leaned down but stopped just an inch away from my lips. "We better make this good," he whispered. I closed my eyes as he narrowed the distance and placed his lips gently on mine.

That was all. He just pressed his lips to mine without moving. I don't know what possessed me to do what I did. I felt his surprise as my lips parted beneath his, and I kissed him back with a little more feeling than I had intended. I could hear his brothers whistling in the background, but all I could think about was how soft his lips were. He stiffened in my arms, and I broke off the kiss in embarrassment. Brian was staring at me blankly.

"Now that's a kiss." Mr. Davis came to slap me on the back. "Good job, young lady. You left him speechless."

I retreated to my place on the couch as the telephone began to ring. Mary went to answer it. "Brian, it's Delilah."

He took the cordless phone from her and quickly left the room as he greeted her. "Hey! How are you?"

Everyone looked back at me, and I looked at the clock. It was after nine at night. I stood up. "I should get going."

They all protested, stressing the dangers of driving at night and the late hour. "I won't hear of it," Mom declared. "Brian, tell her she can't leave at this hour of the night."

He'd come back into the room while I was trying to reason with everyone. "Why would you want to leave now?"

"I don't want to leave, but—"

"Then don't. It's settled. You're staying."

I put my hands on my hips and was about to retort when I felt two little arms wrap around my legs. Little Alissa was looking up at me with her beautiful blue eyes. "Pwease, Aunt Emma. Don't weave. I want you to wead me a bedtime stowy."

My heart melted, and I bent down to take her in my arms, burying my head in her blonde ringlets. She still smelled like a baby. "I'll stay just for you." She threw her arms around my neck and gave me a noisy kiss on the cheek. "How about we go read that story right now?"

She nodded her head vigorously. I carried her upstairs while the mothers did the same with the other children. We got them all dressed for bed and tucked them tightly in their sleeping bags on the floor of one of the bedrooms. When they all settled down, I read *The Poky Little Puppy*. Alissa was asleep before I'd made it halfway through the book. The older ones took a little longer, but they finally all conked out.

"Thanks, Emma," Mary whispered as we left the room. "You're a lifesaver."

"It's my pleasure. They're all so adorable."

"Not all the time," Grace interjected. "But pretty close."

We rejoined the others in the living room and sat up talking and telling stories for a while longer. They'd somehow gotten wind of the Halloween fiasco and insisted that Brian and I tell all the sordid details. I thought his brothers would never quit laughing. Soon the couples started heading upstairs for bed until it was just Brian and I left.

I stood up and stretched. "I think I'll go check on Michelangelo."

"Why don't you go on upstairs? I'll check on him for you."

"Thanks." I hurried upstairs to change into my night-gown and robe before going to the bathroom to wash my face and brush my teeth.

Brian was already in the bed when I got back to the room. He left the lamp on long enough for me to walk to the other side before switching it off. I took off my robe and crawled under the covers. I was careful to stay on my side. His voice came out of the darkness. "What was that all about downstairs?"

"What do you mean?" For a minute, I was puzzled.

"That kiss."

Uh-oh. *Play it cool, Emma.* "What about it?"

"It felt awfully...real."

"You said to make it look good," I said nonchalantly. "So I did. I didn't embarrass you, did I?"

"No, of course not, but what about—"

"How was Delilah?" I broke in. Time for a subject change.

"Great. She asked about you."

"Really?" I couldn't believe it.

"Yeah. I think she's a little envious of the relationship that you have with my family."

More likely she was fiendishly jealous of the time I was spending with him this weekend. "I'm sure they'll love her when they meet her."

"Yeah." He was quiet for a few minutes. "Hey, you don't have any plans for your birthday yet, do you?"

"No."

"Well, keep that night open for me, all right?"

"Okay." I rolled to face him. "What have you got planned?"

"No way. It's a surprise, and I'm not telling no matter how much you beg."

"Fine. I won't try. Good night, Brian."

"Night, Emma." He reached out and ruffled my curls. I silently asked God to keep me on my side of the bed tonight.

I should have asked him to keep Brian on his side too. I awoke to find myself in the same position where I had started, but Brian had migrated to my side sometime during the night and wrapped his right arm around me. I looked down to find that his hand was cupping my left breast. I don't know if I made an abrupt move or what, but his hand tightened its grip for a moment before relaxing again.

Oh God, please don't let him wake up, I prayed as I moved his hand away from my breast and slid out from under his arm. I breathed a sigh of relief as he slept on, and I quickly put on my robe, grabbed some clothes, and retreated to the bathroom. I took a quick, cold shower whether I needed it or not. Someone had used all the hot water.

When I returned to the bedroom, Brian was still lying on the bed. I tiptoed over to my bag and tossed my night-gown and robe inside.

"Good morning."

I slowly turned around, trying not to think about his hand and where it had been. I could feel my face flush any-way. "Good morning."

"Did you leave any hot water?" he asked, indicating my wet hair still wrapped in a towel.

"Actually someone used it all up before I got in."

"Cold?"

I shivered. "Very, but it wakes you up."

"I think I'll pass." He stretched lazily.

"I wouldn't if I were you."

"What's that supposed to mean?" He rolled onto his side and looked at me.

"Nothing," I said coyly. "See you at breakfast."

I walked to the kitchen where Mom was preparing French toast. "Can I help?"

She beamed at me. "Sure. Put on that apron, and you can dip the bread in the egg mixture and plop it on the griddle. I'll flip and stack." We worked in silence for a few minutes until Mom broke it. "How are things progressing between Brian and that Delilah woman?"

"Despite my best efforts, I'm afraid it's progressing rapidly."

"What were your best efforts?"

Blushing a little, I told her about the morning after the Halloween party. "I swear I kept it PG."

"It would have served the rascal right if you had stepped it up to R. It might have taken the blinders off his eyes. Although I think you might have taken a step toward that end last night."

"What do you mean?" I was thinking about the little scene in the bedroom the previous morning.

"I'm talking about that kiss you laid on him last night. His face sure was a sight to behold."

"I felt the way he reacted, Mom. It wasn't enjoyment you were seeing. Repulsion is more like it." It's a good thing I was wearing the apron because I plopped that piece on the griddle a little too hard.

"Emma, don't be so hard on yourself. You don't give yourself half the credit you deserve."

"Thanks, Mom." We finished cooking the toast and set the stacks on the table. I got out the powdered sugar and maple syrup while she called everyone to breakfast. They filed in and took seats at the table. I noticed Brian's hair was wet. He'd taken a cold shower after all.

Alissa came running over to me. "Can I sit wiff you, Aunt Emma?"

"You sure can." I lifted her onto my lap. "Do you want powdered sugar or syrup on your toast?"

"Sywup." It wasn't long before she'd had enough. "I'm done." Her face and hands were a sticky mess.

"Let's go get you cleaned up."

"I'll take her, Emma." Mary had come around the table to get her. "You finish your breakfast."

I watched Alissa trot along beside her mother before turning back to my breakfast. It was delicious even when cold. I don't think there was anything Mom couldn't cook. After everyone had finished, all of us girls gathered in the kitchen to help with the dishes. It didn't take long with the six of us.

I went upstairs to retrieve my bag and left it in the hallway as I walked into the living room. I gave Mom a hug. "Thank you for having me this weekend, but I really must be going."

She hugged me tightly. "I know, but I hate to see you go. You know you're welcome anytime."

When I gave Mr. Davis a big bear hug of my own, he asked, "You're coming back for Christmas, aren't you?"

I looked over to where Brian was talking to Andrew. If he started bringing Delilah with him, I wasn't sure how much longer I'd feel comfortable being here. "We'll see, Dad." I gave him another hug.

Brian walked over to us. "I'll follow you home, Emma."

"You don't have to do that, Brian. You should stay and spend more time with your family."

"I know I don't have to, but this way I can make sure you get home all right. Besides, I've got to be getting back too." No doubt he had a date with Delilah that evening, I thought.

I said my good-byes to everyone else as Brian got his things together. When they followed us into the hall, I started out the door but noticed Brian looking up at the ceiling and backing a few feet away. "Are you coming?"

"You go ahead."

I looked up at the ceiling and saw that Andrew had moved the mistletoe. He was sweet to have tried, but it only made it clear that Brian didn't want to be anywhere near my lips again. I looked back at him, then turned without a word and walked to my car.

Mr. Davis had already gotten Michelangelo into the backseat with the turkey bone. As soon as I was buckled in, I gave a final wave and drove away without waiting for Brian. I didn't need his help getting home. I was a thoroughly capable driver, and I had retrieved my gun from under the seat where I had hidden it. Who needed a man?

Chapter Fourteen

I STOPPED AT the local coffee shop on the way into work Monday morning. Kathy and I were going to need all the caffeine we could get in order to make it through the next few weeks. The month of December was always our busiest time at the bookstore, with last-minute shoppers picking up gifts for the children in their families.

Kathy was beaming when I walked through the door.

"You must have had a good weekend," I greeted her.

"Oh, Emma." She clasped her hands together dramatically and whirled around on her toes. "It was perfect. They were so nice, and they made me feel right at home."

"I knew you had nothing to worry about."

She looked liked she'd just taken a bite of the world's best chocolate. "His mom paid me the greatest compliment. She said she's never seen Donnie this happy before."

"I could say the same about you." She was practically glowing. "It must be a match made in heaven."

"His mother hung some mistletoe, and Donnie kissed me under it." She was hugging herself now, and I thought her face would split from the big smile stretched across it. "Emma, he told me he loves me."

"That's wonderful, Kathy. Did you say it back?" I looked at her expectantly, knowing the answer already by the smile on her face. I couldn't help but wish that my kiss under the mistletoe had turned out differently.

"I most certainly did and got a roll in the hay into the bargain." She wiggled her eyebrows.

"You're so bad." Laughing, I gave her a hug. "Well, you deserve to be happy." I turned to the register to make sure we had enough cash on hand.

"Thanks. How about your weekend?" She started refilling the candy jar.

"Well, it was somewhat like yours actually. There was a kiss under the mistletoe, but I definitely did not get an 'I love you' from Brian or a roll in the hay exactly." My thoughts strayed for a moment as I closed the drawer.

"What?" she gasped. "Explain. Quickly. I want all the details." She sat on a stool behind the counter and focused on me intently.

I told her all about my weekend and ended with the mistletoe incident. "I think I completely screwed up. I should never have kissed him like that."

"Honey, fate handed you an opportunity, and you took it." She walked over to give me a comforting embrace. "No one can fault you for that, but judging from his reaction, it was probably a good thing that you played it off as a joke."

"Yeah." Even I could hear the dejection in my voice. "Tell me more about your weekend. I'm tired of thinking about mine."

"Well—" She was off and running until the customers came in droves.

The next few days flew by in a flurry of activity at the bookstore and even more hectic evenings as I tried to finish my own Christmas shopping. I was struggling with what to get Brian. I'd seen him a little more frequently during the last week because Delilah was always off to some conference or other. Steve had been called away to Chicago, so I hadn't had to try to keep him at bay. However, the time Brian and I spent together had become awkward. He kept looking at me as if he expected me to pounce on him at any moment.

He was still going to take me out for my birthday, however. He wouldn't say what he had planned, but he was picking me up on Saturday at six o'clock. He'd suggested western attire, which had me a little worried. He'd also told me to bring only my keys and driver's license. It was all very curious.

My birthday. The family celebration would consist of cake and presents at Sunday dinner, which was usually fun until Mother started worrying about my biological clock. It didn't bother me that I was getting older. I sometimes still felt like I was just fresh out of high school. Time certainly flew fast.

I'd received another e-mail from John. His mother had made a full recovery, and he was planning to be in Dallas on the twelfth. We'd made plans to have dinner and left the rest of the evening open.

I had never seen Brian look more handsome than when I opened my door on Saturday night. He was in Wranglers and a long-sleeved western shirt with ostrich-skin boots and a black felt cowboy hat.

"You should do the cowboy look more often," I told him.

"Thanks." He looked me over from head to toe. "You don't look half bad yourself, pardner." I also was wearing Wranglers and boots—no hat, though. "You ready to go?"

"All set." I grabbed my keys from the bar, and we were out the door.

Our first stop was our favorite barbeque restaurant. We chowed down on ribs and sauce with peach cobbler à la mode for dessert. It was fantastic. He paid the check, and we headed back to the car. "Where to next?" I asked curiously.

He gave me a huge grin. "I'm taking you dancing."

"That's great!" I loved dancing. "Where?"

The grin was wider now. "Billy Bob's."

I glanced at him in surprise. "I've never been there."

He gave me a little wink and answered, "I know."

It was crowded and loud, but I loved every bit of it. I almost fainted when Keith Urban walked out on stage to perform. "You didn't tell me he was going to be here!" I yelled into Brian's ear to be heard over the applause and shouting. I was bouncing up and down with excitement. Keith was by far my favorite country singer. His songs could either lift you up or rip your heart out.

"That's my birthday present to you," he shouted back.

I gave him a huge hug and turned back to the stage as Keith began to play "Somebody Like You." Everyone was clapping and singing along to the music. He certainly put on a great show. He ended with "Your Everything," and couples all around us began dancing slowly with the music. Brian took my hand in his and pulled me to him. I rested my head on his shoulder and followed his lead, wishing the night would never end.

Unfortunately it did. Everyone gave a final round of applause, and Brian and I made our way to the exit. I took his hand and clasped it tightly. "I'll never forget this, Brian. Thank you."

Satisfaction was written all over his face. "I knew you'd love it."

We rode in silence for a while as Brian drove toward home. "So where's Delilah tonight?" I kept my voice neutral, but I was really dying to know what she had said about his taking me out tonight.

"Girls' night out with her friends." He said it matter-of-factly with no hint of disappointment or any other emotion, for that matter.

I tried again. "She's been a busy girl the last few weeks with all those conferences."

"Yes, she has." Still nothing.

I decided to take the plunge. "So how are things going with you two?"

I should have remembered that curiosity killed the cat. "I'm taking her to meet my parents for Christmas," he said. A hint of anxiety had made it into his tone.

I sat in silent despair as my heart ripped in two. He had to be serious about her if he was taking her home for Christmas. I closed my eyes against the tears and tried to swallow the lump in my throat. I had to say something. "That's great." I didn't sound convincing, so I tried something else. "Have you told them?"

"Not yet, but I will soon." He sighed. "Mom would never forgive me if I didn't give her time to make sure everything's perfect."

I somehow managed to listen to him talk about his plans for the holidays without hyperventilating or letting him know that anything was wrong, but I was completely devastated. Any hope I might have had of his ever loving me was gone. My fate as a spinster was truly sealed.

I was relieved when he pulled into his driveway. He walked me to my door. I tried to look at him, but it just hurt too much. I concentrated on opening the door. "Thanks for tonight, Brian. I'll never forget it." That was an understatement. His words were forever seared into my brain.

"You're welcome, Emma." No usual peck on the cheek or hug. Nothing. He just turned away into the darkness.

I shut and locked my door behind me without another word, heading straight for my bedroom to let the air out of Cary, where he'd been hanging out in my reading chair, before hiding him out of sight in the closet. I couldn't look at it again.

I walked to my dresser and pulled Brian's sweatshirt from it. I had never returned it to him. I took it to the laundry room and set it aside as I started the washing machine on a short cycle. I added detergent and picked up the sweatshirt, burying my face in it one last time and breathing deeply of the scent it still held. Forcing my hands to unclench, I let it fall into the water and slammed the lid shut.

The tears finally won out, and I slid to the floor sobbing until a shell of numbness began to build itself around my heart. By the time the washer clicked off, I was calm. I rose stiffly from the floor to put the sweatshirt in the dryer. I'd return it to him tomorrow.

I let Michelangelo in from the backyard and pulled off my clothes. I went into the bathroom and took a dose of Nyquil. It never failed to knock me out, and I needed oblivion. I didn't have to face the reality of my shattered heart while sleeping. I fell into bed, and eventually a merciful darkness enveloped me. I didn't wake up until my phone rang the next morning.

"Hello?" I felt and sounded lifeless.

"Emma? Are you okay? Why aren't you here yet?" It was Mother.

"Where's here?" I mumbled.

"Church. It's after eleven."

I looked at my clock. It was five after to be exact. My internal alarm had failed again. I hadn't even thought about church last night, but even if I had, I wouldn't have gone today. I couldn't take seeing Brian with Delilah knowing his intentions. Not yet. I needed time for the numbness to be complete.

"Emma, are you still there?"

"I'm sorry, Mother. I'm just not feeling well this morning." Another understatement.

"What's wrong?"

"I hurt all over, and my stomach's upset." That was definitely the truth.

"Well, you certainly sound terrible."

"Thanks."

"Go back to sleep. I'll check on you later." She hung up.

I went back to bed but not to sleep. I was depressed and moping, and I hated it. Later, the doorbell rang, and I put on my robe to answer it. I opened the door to find the last two people I wanted to see right now.

"How are you feeling?" Brian asked with concern.

"Fine." I sounded robotic. I didn't invite them in.

"You look like you feel terrible," Delilah said sweetly. It was her way of saying I looked terrible, but I didn't care. It didn't matter anymore.

"I have something for you, Brian. Stay there a second." I retrieved the sweatshirt from the dryer. "Sorry I took so long to return it." I shoved it at him.

"I'd completely forgotten it." He looked surprised and then tried to hand it back to me. "Why don't you just keep it?"

"No thanks." I wrapped my arms around my waist to resist the temptation. "I have plenty of sweatshirts. If y'all don't mind, I'm going back to bed."

"Of course," he said. "We just wanted to check on you. Do you need anything?"

I shrugged. "Nope, I have everything I need."

"Well, I'll check on you later."

I shook my head. I wasn't going to be dependent any longer. "That's not necessary. I'll be fine." I shut the door and went back to bed and moped without any more interruptions.

Kathy took one look at me as I came dragging into the bookstore and hurried over. "What's wrong?" she asked.

I grimaced. "Do I look that terrible?"

She nodded. "You look like death warmed over."

"Just the look I was going for," I said brightly.

She marched me behind the counter and sat me on the stool. "You look like you're about to pass out. Now what's the matter?"

I slouched over onto the counter, my head cradled in my arms. "He's taking her to meet his parents." I didn't have to explain who I was talking about.

I could see the tears in her eyes. She was a very empathetic person. "Oh, honey." She took me in her arms, and I sat there stiffly. "I'm so sorry. When did you find out?"

"On my birthday, on the way home from Billy Bob's where he had taken me dancing and to see Keith Urban sing." I pulled away from her and started tidying the counter.

"That's terrible. Do his parents know?"

I shook my head mutely.

"His mother's going to crap bricks."

I nodded dumbly.

"I don't know what to say, Emma."

I kept right on tidying. "There's nothing *to* say. I've just got to move on without him."

She looked like she was going to say something else. I spoke before she could. "Let's get to work."

A short time later, the bell jingled over the door, and we looked up to find Brian standing hesitantly in the doorway. "Brian!" I exclaimed, shocked to see him there. He walked over to where I was standing behind the counter and took my hand without saying a word. It was trembling.

Something was wrong, terribly wrong. There were tears in his eyes, and his jaw was working as if he wanted to speak but couldn't. "Brian, what's the matter?" I asked in growing concern. I looked at Kathy, but she looked as stunned as I did.

"Sit down, Emma," he finally managed.

I sat, a horrible fear washing over me. I grabbed his other hand. "Brian, you're scaring me. What is wrong?" I started panicking as my thoughts flew to Anne and the baby. "Is something wrong with Anne, with the baby?" He shook his head. "Mother? Dad?" I stood up and started for the phone, but he pulled me back.

"No, Emma. I'm sorry for scaring you. Nothing's wrong with your family."

I sat back down in relief and looked him straight in the eye. "Then what is wrong?"

"It's about Steve."

"Steve?" I asked, trying to figure out what could make Brian cry about Steve.

"I caught him with another woman. Red-handed," he said gently.

I heard a sharp intake of breath from Kathy, but I just chuckled cynically. "Is that all?" As soon as I looked at his eyes, a light bulb went off. "You caught him with Delilah, didn't you?" I asked quietly.

His face registered his surprise. "How did you know?"

"I don't know; it just popped into my head about all her conferences and his meetings being in Chicago and something he said once." Realizing exactly how he must be feeling, I stood up and put my arms around him. "Brian, I'm so sorry."

Kathy discreetly disappeared as he asked, "You're not upset?"

I leaned back far enough to look into his eyes, framing his face with my hands. "Only for you."

I held him close and tried to comfort him as best I could. Finally he stepped back a little and said, "I just can't believe how blind I was."

I gave his hand a little shake. "Hey, everybody's blind when they're in love." He looked at me thoughtfully for a minute but didn't say anything. I took his arm. "Come on. Let's get out of here and go eat a pint of ice cream and watch a movie. What'll it be? Arnold, Mel, Steven, or Harrison?"

He squeezed my arm. "You're the best, Emma."

I squeezed him back and grinned. "What are friends for?"

Chapter Fifteen

I SPENT AS much time as possible with Brian during the next few days just trying to be there for him as he had been for me. He was definitely hurt and embarrassed that he hadn't been able to see through Delilah's act, but he wasn't completely devastated either. I had several conversations with his mother, and we both finally convinced him to visit the ranch that weekend. I saw him off Friday evening and crashed thankfully into bed, but not before letting everyone in the family know just what a prick Steve was.

By the time Saturday evening arrived, I was wishing I had canceled my dinner plans with John, but Kathy wouldn't let me. "You need a distraction. Go out and try to have fun."

He picked me up at six and took me to La Madeleine. He ordered a bottle of wine, and I couldn't help but think about my last blind date that involved a bottle of wine. I must have made a strange face at that because as the waitress stepped away, he asked, "You don't mind, do you?"

"Mind what?" I asked in confusion.

"My ordering the wine. You frowned as if you disapproved."

I laughed then. "I'm so sorry. No, I don't mind. It was just thinking of my last blind date; it was horrible."

He smiled warmly. "What happened?"

"It started with his drinking two bottles of wine with dinner and ended with a wrestling match." I shivered as I remembered my fear.

He looked at me with something I couldn't quite put my finger on, but thankfully moved on to other topics. He wanted me to try the escargot, but I refused. "Sorry, but antenna freak me out." He just laughed and finished them off.

I let him do most of the talking during dinner. He told me about the places he had traveled to since I had last seen him and all the collectibles he had procured. I could see how much he enjoyed his work.

After we'd finished dessert, he took my hand across the table. "You've been awfully quiet this evening." He looked concerned.

I pulled my hand back across the table. "I'm sorry, John. It's been a busy week at work, and I guess I'm just a little tired." *Exhausted* would have been a better word. "You said you had some business to discuss with me?"

"Could we discuss it at your bookstore? I've been wanting to see it." He paid the check, and we were on our way. It wasn't long before we were at the store. I led the way in and started to place my purse on the counter, but the click of the deadbolt sliding into place stopped me. I turned.

I never saw it coming. His fist shattered my nose, and I felt the blood pouring down my face as I stumbled backward. The pain was excruciating, and blood was pounding in my ears. I screamed.

The second blow caught me just below my right eye. I felt something sharp against my skin and the trickle of blood again as I fell backwards. Something snapped when I fell on my left arm. My head had hit the counter on the way down, and a black mist began to gather in my peripheral vision. I shook my head to try and clear it but got an instant headache instead. I fell over onto my stomach with my purse a hard bulge underneath me.

I must have blacked out for a while because I woke to hear things being thrown around. Then I heard his voice cold as steel in my ear. "Where are the books, Emma?"

I was terrified. I couldn't pass out again. "What?"

He sent a kick flying into my side. "Don't play dumb with me."

I was gasping for breath, pain stabbing like a knife with each one, but it felt like I couldn't get any air. I tried to focus and slow my breathing because the pain was threatening to pull me into blackness again.

I couldn't tell him where the books were because it would only make him angrier. The fog lifted from my brain for a second, and I realized that the bulge in my purse was my gun. I just had to reach it.

"They're in my office. I'll get them. Just don't hit me again." I tried to rise, but he'd already grabbed my left arm and rolled me onto my back. I fought against a scream as the pain radiated all over. My arm was definitely broken, but I couldn't let him know I was hurt.

He was sitting on my thighs. "You're lying!" he hissed. "I've already searched this place from top to bottom!" He punched me again, and stars exploded behind my eyes. I heard the buttons plink across the room as he ripped my shirt open, but I was too dazed to react. I could feel the goose bumps rise on my skin from the coolness of the air. "I have ways of getting at the truth, Emma," he whispered in my ear.

The blackness was still hovering, and it didn't help that I couldn't get a deep breath. I heard another click and felt cold metal swiftly leave a searing cut across the top of my left breast, and it sent the blackness flying.

"That woke you up, didn't it?" he sneered. "Now where are they?" He was holding a knife.

Dazed, I answered. "They're at the bank in a safe deposit box."

"Well, well. The bank won't open until morning, so what are we going to do with all this time before us?" He chuckled softly as he slid the knife between my bra and my breastbone. There was a sharp tug, and some of the restriction eased around my chest. He touched the point of it to my throat as the fingers of his other hand trailed around my breasts. My skin crawled at his touch. "Since such a wonderful opportunity has presented itself, let's have some fun."

I was desperately trying to think of how to get free as his exploring hand found the waist of my skirt. The knife left my throat to cut it. Miraculously I realized my right hand was still clutching my purse. I slowly eased my hand into the purse and gripped my gun, clicking the safety off. Adrenaline pulsed through my veins as I lifted my right hand to his shoulder—purse, gun, and all—and fired.

I tried to blink back the darkness as the knife plunged downward. He fell off me, clutching his bloody shoulder and cursing. I looked down and saw the knife protruding from my left side. I almost fainted then, but somehow I managed to scoot away from him until I felt my back press against the bar. I took a second to pull the phone off the counter by its cord before pointing the gun dead center of his chest, my hand now steady as a rock. I was hurting, badly, but I wasn't about to let him see it. I prayed to God that he would just stay down. I didn't want to kill him, but I would if he came at me again.

"Make one move toward me, and I'll shoot you dead." My voice left no doubt that I meant what I said. Curled up on his undamaged side, he glared at me as best he could with pain-glazed eyes, but I saw the fear in them too. I put the phone to my ear and dialed 911 on the keypad with my gun hand. Then I aimed the gun back at him.

"Nine-one-one. What is your emergency?" the dispatcher's familiar voice answered. Sue Dayton had known me since I was a baby.

I took a shallow breath to speak. "Sue, this is Emma Bailey. I've just shot an intruder in my store." I kept my eyes and gun focused on him.

"Hold on, Emma. I'm sending the police and an ambulance now." I could hear her sending out the call.

"Better make it two," I answered through gritted teeth. The blackness was threatening again, and I couldn't breathe well. I could feel the sticky warmth of my own blood as it trickled down my side.

I heard a gasp. "Are you hurt?"

"Yes." I was feeling clammy and cold.

"Where? How bad?" I could hear the mounting concern in her voice, but I couldn't be specific. I didn't want John to get any ideas about trying to fight me because I was wounded.

Instead I answered, "He's conscious, but I shot him in the shoulder at point-blank range."

She read between the lines. "I understand, Emma." Her voice had become dead calm, and I knew she did it for my sake. "You're afraid to tell me because he can hear what you're saying. I'm going to stay on the line with you until the police arrive. You should be hearing the sirens any time now."

"I can hear them coming down the street." Spots were dancing in my vision, but I couldn't give up yet. I shook my head, and it pounded, but at least the spots receded. "Tell them the deadbolt's locked, so they'll have to break in."

"Will do."

I heard the sound of breaking glass, and I was so thankful because my eyes were trying to close against my will. I felt someone near me. "Emma?" Someone was trying to pry the gun from my hand. "Emma, can you hear me? Where's that ambulance? She's not responding!"

Then I heard someone yelling, "Emma! Emma!" I thought I recognized the voice. I tried to see who it was, but the spots were obstructing my view.

Brian had forced his way into the store and ran toward me. "Brian," I sighed as he reached me and the black mist finally covered my eyes.

❧

My memories of that evening and the next couple of days were sketchy due to the blow to my head and the mercies of pain medication. I had flashes of Brian in the ambulance and the doctor's examination in the emergency room, but there were many blanks that I couldn't fill before and after. The doctor assured me that it was normal to have some memory loss from the concussion, but unfortunately I remembered the painful parts. Not only did I have a concussion and a broken arm, but the kick to my side had also broken some ribs, one of which had caused a lung to partially collapse. As a result, I now had a chest tube inserted to help re-inflate it. Luckily the knife hadn't done any major damage, just a flesh wound that hurt every time I moved.

The doctor came to set the bones in my arm, and as he pulled, I couldn't help but cry out with the pain and then the overwhelming nausea. Through the haze, I saw Brian leave the room. He only returned once the bones in my arm had been set, but he never left my bed again as they stitched up the cuts.

My family had come to the hospital as soon as Brian had called. I'm afraid they suffered some very anxious hours before I was coherent enough to answer questions. Their relief was palpable when I answered that John had not raped me as the state of my clothing had suggested, but they were still mad as hell. Two cops were in the hallway trying to restrain Dad and Teddy from paying John a visit in his own ER room. Brian never left my side.

My nose was going to need some work, but the swelling had to recede first. I had two black eyes, the right one swollen shut. Because of the partially collapsed lung, I would be in the hospital until the chest tube did its job, which the doctor said should take no more than five days. I spent a lot of the time sleeping, but it wasn't always restful or comfortable. I suffered from nightmares and often woke sweaty with my heart pounding.

Brian refused to leave the hospital. I had been moved out of the ER into a private room, and he was at my bedside every time the nurses would let him, as was the rest of the family. He just sat there quietly while I was sleeping,

I guess, because he was almost always there to answer my questions about what had happened when I was awake. Dad finally ordered him to go home and get some rest when he fell asleep in the chair by my bed. He slept on a couch in the waiting room instead.

Teddy had already taken Anne home, so Mother took over when Brian went to sleep. She was in her element, being the devoted mother and harassing the nurses. I know she loved me, but her dramatics quickly became annoying. Over the next couple of days, Anne, Kathy, and Brian helped to keep me from going stark, raving mad.

When Mother started talking about taking me to the parsonage after I left the hospital, I began to get panicky. Dad somehow managed to drag her away for a little while when Kathy came to visit again.

"Kathy, you've got to do me a favor," I begged her. "When they release me, will you come stay with me?"

She looked confused. "Of course, but your mother said—"

"I don't care what she said. I can't be at home by myself, but I can't stay with her either. I'll kill her or myself before the first day is over."

She looked at me for a moment before asking, "What about Brian?"

I looked at the empty chair where Brian had sat earlier. "Much as I might love to stay with Brian, I don't think he could take being steamrolled by my mother right now. She'd never let us stay that long together alone without a chaperone. Not after the handcuff incident." I couldn't help but laugh at the thought, but I quickly stopped because the pain was unbearable.

She patted my hand. "I wouldn't be so sure about that."

I was. "Please just say you'll do it."

"You know I will, honey. Don't you worry." She smiled and gave my hand another pat. "I'll take care of everything."

They were releasing me tomorrow. The doctor had removed the chest tube earlier that morning, which was a strange experience, to say the least. An officer came to visit me that evening and gave me an update on what they had learned about John. Because his gunshot wound had not been very serious, he'd been in jail since the morning after he attacked me.

The officer informed me that John was a career thief who specialized in obtaining valuable items for unscrupulous collectors. The weekend he'd supposedly been called to his mother's sickbed, he'd actually perpetrated a theft. "He's also got a history of violence against his victims. Compared to some of them, you're very lucky, ma'am. He's always been able to elude the authorities until now. Thanks to you, he'll be rotting behind bars for quite a while."

I didn't feel lucky. I felt stupid. I should have listened to my instincts about him and stayed far, far away.

My final morning in the hospital was not pleasant. The swelling in my nose had gone down enough to assess the damage. An otolaryngologist was called in, and although it didn't require surgery, he had to manipulate my nose to get everything back in place. Then he put it in a splint and scheduled a follow-up appointment. Brian was there holding my hand the entire time. It was only a week until Christmas, and I couldn't help but wonder what I had done to earn this lump of coal in my stocking.

Mother was not at all happy to find that I had made other arrangements for my recovery, but Kathy would not let her bully me. I had picked the perfect gatekeeper. She and Brian would drive me home.

In spite of their protests, I made them take me by the store. They helped me up the sidewalk to the front door, and I closed my eyes against the rushing onslaught of memories and the feeling of terror they brought. Kathy patted my back when I quickly bent over with hands on my knees.

Brian was at my side in a second. "Emma, you're trembling. Are you sure you want to do this now?"

I shook my head, waiting for the nausea and cold sweat to pass. "I refuse to let him beat me." I stood upright, gripped the doorknob firmly, and swung the door wide, taking a step inside. I knew that Anne, Teddy, and Kathy had been here before me to clean the place up, but images from that night were swirling before my eyes in dizzying momentum. I could still feel the blows and felt a moment of irrational fear at the thought of turning around. My knees buckled, but Brian caught me up in his arms gingerly.

"Come on, babe." I shut my eyes and hid my face in the curve of his neck as he held me tighter. "We'll do this later."

I didn't protest as he carried me back to the car, and Kathy locked up. When we arrived at my house, he carried me into the bedroom and waited while Kathy pulled the covers down on the bed. He set me down gently and tucked the covers around me before sitting down on the edge of the bed. I opened my eyes as he tucked a stray curl behind my ear. He looked so tired and concerned, I just wanted to kiss it all away and make it better.

Kathy was standing there looking concerned. "How're you doing?"

I took a deep breath and broke eye contact with Brian. "I'll be okay." I heard a scratch at the back door. Kathy went to let Michelangelo inside to greet me with ecstatic tail wagging and hand licking. I patted his head. "I've missed you too, buddy."

Kathy went to the kitchen to fix us a late lunch, and Mike settled on the floor by the bed. I turned back to Brian. He was looking out the window, but I could see tears glistening in his eyes. "Hey," I whispered. He turned back to look at me, and I reached out a hand to wipe his cheek. "I'm okay, Brian. I promise."

He caught my hand and pressed a kiss to my palm. "I was so scared, Emma. I left the ranch early because I just had a feeling that I needed to see you, and when I drove through town and saw the ambulances at the store, I thought I'd lost you." His voice broke.

I patted the bed next to me. "Come here, Brian." He eased up beside me and took me gently in his arms. "See, you didn't lose me. I'm still here, although I'm not looking my best." Catching a glimpse of myself in the mirror above my dresser, I was not a pretty sight. The swelling in my eye had gone down, but the swelling around my nose was back thanks to the doctor's manipulations that morning. Plus I looked like a raccoon with the bruising around my eyes.

He chuckled softly. "You're beautiful." I rested my head on his chest and let the beating of his heart lull me to sleep.

John was on top of me cutting the names of my books into my chest. I struggled to reach my gun as he raised the knife above his head. I screamed as it plunged downward and kept screaming as it plunged again and again.

"Emma! Emma!" Brian was shaking me awake. "Wake up. It's just a nightmare."

I threw myself into his arms, my teeth chattering and body shaking uncontrollably. "Don't leave me again," I sobbed. "Please don't leave me."

He held me close and rubbed my back soothingly. "Shh, it's all right. I'll never leave you."

Chapter Sixteen

FOR THE NEXT week, Brian, Kathy, and sometimes Donnie kept me entertained in the evenings. Kathy was sleeping on the couch so that Brian could stay with me during the night. I was still having nightmares, and he was determined to keep his word. Mother and the rest of the family checked in daily through phone calls or short visits. If it became too overwhelming, all I had to do was yawn, and everyone scurried away.

During the day while everyone was at work, I had a lot of time to think over everything that had happened during the last few months. I had been happy again after the breakup with Steve when I found a friend in Brian. Everything had gone south when I had let friendship turn into something more, on my side at least, but I was working through that, and Brian and I were better friends than ever.

We spent a lot of time talking and getting to know each other again during the wee hours after I'd had yet another nightmare. He could always distract me with some story about his childhood or lull me back to sleep by trying to explain computer networking.

Before we knew it, Christmas Eve dawned cold and clear. I was just going to throw on some comfortable clothes to go to the parsonage, especially considering how hard it still was for me to get around, but Kathy wouldn't hear of it.

"Come on. I'll do your hair and try to diminish the bruises as much as possible. It's Christmas Eve. Everyone should look festive and beautiful." She looked like the cat that ate the canary as she bustled around me, but no amount of questioning on my part led to any reasonable answers.

Nothing was going to hide the bruises, but I did look much better by the time she'd gotten through with me. "You're a miracle worker, Kathy." I gave her a one-armed hug. "Thanks."

"You're welcome. Now let's get to that fabulous dinner your mother has prepared." I had invited Kathy and Donnie to join us. Brian had left earlier for his parents' house, and I already missed him. We drove to the parsonage, and they got me settled on the couch. Uncle Richard was the only one to make tacky comments about my appearance hurting my love life. Everyone else kept their mouths shut for once.

We exchanged and opened gifts, knowing that the kids would never settle down to dinner if we didn't. After the last gift was opened, my father stood up. "Before we go to the dining room, someone would like to make an announcement."

I turned to see Brian. He started weaving his way toward me through my family as Kathy just stood there with tears in her eyes and a giddy smile. Donnie went to her side and put his arm around her.

"What are you doing here?" I asked in confusion as Brian reached me. "I thought you'd gone to your parents."

He took both my hands in his and helped me up to stand beside him. "I had a little shopping to do first."

"What for?"

"For you." He smiled as he knelt beside the couch and took a little blue velvet jeweler's box from his pocket.

He opened the lid, and the diamond ring glittered in the light. Everything and everyone else faded away as he spoke the words I longed to hear. "I love you, Emma Katherine Bailey."

I looked into his eyes and saw nothing but love. It was true. He really did love me. Tears of happiness slid down my cheeks, and he stood to wipe them away with his thumbs. I managed, "I love you too."

He took the ring from the box and leaned his head against mine. Taking a deep breath, he whispered, "Marry me?"

"Yes!" I whispered back, nodding and laughing as he slipped the ring on my finger.

His eyes traveled to my lips, and I closed my eyes in anticipation of his kiss, but it didn't come. I opened my eyes and saw the desire in his. "I want to kiss you, but I don't want to hurt you either."

"Kiss me anyway." I giggled nervously. "If it hurts, I'll know it's real." Our lips met, and this time all the love and desire I felt for him was returned in his kiss.

Everyone was clapping and hollering in the background, Uncle Richard loudest of all. "I knew she'd land her a good one!" he yelled.

I was beginning to feel dizzy, whether from his kiss or from having stood too long, I wasn't sure. I grabbed the front of Brian's sweater with my right hand as my knees buckled, and I swayed toward him.

He caught me before I fell and lifted me up into his arms. "Emma!" He sounded terrified.

I put my good arm around his neck. "I'm fine, Brian. Now that you're here, I'm fine."

Mother had appeared at his side. "Take her into the bedroom, Brian. She's probably been up too long and needs to lie down a while."

He held me close as he walked to the bedroom and gently placed me on the bed, kneeling beside me and smoothing the hair away from my face. I'd lived this moment before. "You really did kiss me that night, didn't you? The night after I fell asleep at church, when you came to check on me."

He smiled. "Yes. I'd wanted to for a long time, and you were so beautiful lying there asleep, I couldn't resist. Are you okay now? Do you need me to get you anything?" He was looking concerned again.

I grabbed the front of his sweater and pulled him toward me. "Kiss me until I'm dizzy again." He complied with gusto until we were both breathless and more than a little disheveled.

I moved over to let him sit on the bed. He smiled and pulled me closer. "I seem to be having some déjà vu," he said as he ran his hands up my back and into my hair. "I would have kissed you that morning at my parents' if we hadn't been interrupted."

"I desperately wanted you to, but what about Delilah?"

"I was only dating her because I thought I didn't stand a chance with you."

"What do you mean?" I asked in surprise.

"Well, I kept trying little things to see if you felt the same way I did, but you'd just freeze me. Then I decided to just tell you and let the chips fall where they may. You remember that morning I came over to tell you that you weren't pathetic?" I nodded and cringed at the memory. "I had actually come over to tell you how much I loved you, but you made it perfectly clear that you didn't want to hear anything I had to say."

I grabbed a fistful of shirt and shook it. "You fool! I was so in love with you already, and I was terrified that you were going to tell me something awful, like that you were in love with Delilah. Why didn't you just blurt it out instead of beating around the bush?"

He chuckled and gave me another kiss before settling back against the pillows. "When did you first realize that you loved me?" he asked, nuzzling his nose in my hair.

"The first morning you brought Delilah to church. I woke up in your arms and realized how much I loved you. Then you had to go and ruin it by mentioning her." I huffed for a moment before asking, "When did you know you loved me?"

He moved so that he could look into my face. "The first time I laid eyes on you." He shook his head. "All this time we've wasted apart over silly miscommunication. Let's promise each other that from now on we'll tell each other everything. No secrets."

"You've got it," and I sealed that promise with a kiss.

He was laughing now. "To that purpose, I have to admit that I wasn't asleep the morning I, uh, groped your breast."

My mouth dropped open, and I hit him in the arm with my fist. I leaned forward and whispered into his ear, "Too bad you played possum. I might have let you do more than that if you'd just asked."

"Really?" He waggled his eyebrows.

"I guess you'll never know now."

"We'll see about that." He wrapped his arms around me and pulled me down beside him. Careful not to bump my injured arm or hold me too tight, he leaned over to kiss me. I grabbed his butt.

He leaned back to look at me. "What are you doing?"

I chuckled. "A little groping of my own. It's the best I can do with one hand."

His face took on a mischievous grin, and my pulse started racing as he undid one of the buttons on my blouse. His hand moved to the next one. "What do you think you're doing?" It came out a little breathless. He was already to the third button.

"I'm looking to see if you're wearing that red lingerie again."

"Oh, you!"

His fingers trailed across the angry red scar where John had cut me. He leaned down to kiss it before looking deeply into my eyes. "I promise, Emma. I'll make it all better." I pulled him down for another kiss.

We both turned in surprise as the door opened. "Emma, I came to check...." Mother's words trailed off as she took in the scene before her. "I see you're feeling better. Dinner is ready." She turned and shut the door behind her.

Brian and I both started laughing. "Uh-oh. You're going to have to make an honest woman of me now."

"With pleasure." He held me close and kissed me again before sitting me up and buttoning my blouse. "Are you sorry you're giving up spinsterhood?"

"It was a nice idea for a time, but it can't beat living the rest of my days with you. And nights," I added mischievously.

He took my hand and helped me stand. "I can guarantee that. Let's go join our engagement party."

It was the happiest day of my life.

Epilogue

SIX MONTHS LATER, I was standing at the back of the church yet again as music floated from the organ. I turned to Kathy. "Ready?" She nodded her head, and I walked through the door of the sanctuary where Brian was waiting to take my arm on the other side. Kathy was the bride today, and I was her matron of honor.

Brian and I had been married three months before by my father at our favorite spot in the park where we had watched the shooting stars. It was a beautiful ceremony, and our families could not have been happier at the turn of events.

As we progressed down the aisle, he leaned down and whispered, "Remember our wedding night?"

I felt the heat rise to my cheeks as I nodded. "I expect a repeat performance tonight."

"Your wish is my command," he said as we parted and took our places.

The "Bridal Chorus" began, and a radiant Kathy met a beaming Donnie at the altar. As Dad walked them through the traditional ceremony, I couldn't take my eyes off my handsome husband. He had made me the happiest woman in the world. I couldn't wait until tonight when I could tell him that I would be declaring motherhood.

About the Author

Chata Segich of Born Again Images, 2010

Born in Fort Worth, Texas, Jamie Lynn Braziel attended Southeastern Oklahoma State University, where she majored in English and minored in French. A financial analyst, the author is working toward a master's degree in accounting.